SPORTING MOUSTACHES

AUG STONE

ILLUSTRATIONS BY

ALLEN CRAWFORD

Some of these stories first appeared, sometimes in different form, in the journals *Vol. 1 Brooklyn* and *Exacting Clam*.

Set in Mrs Eaves with LaTeX.

ISBN: 978-1-952386-80-0 (paperback)
ISBN: 978-1-952386-81-7 (ebook)
Library of Congress Control Number: 2023948178

Sagging Meniscus Press
Montclair, New Jersey
saggingmeniscus.com

For my Dad

from whom I get my sense of humor

and who has always had a moustache

CONTENTS

Sporting Moustaches

Let Us Begin

Years later, after he had long since retired from the game that would lovingly dominate his life, when he had taken to reading the works of the eminent Swiss psychoanalyst Carl Gustav Jung in the evenings before retiring to bed, Gordon Mathieu finally found in 'synchronicity' the word for the momentous events that had coalesced on March 4, 1875 and thus set the course for his career. After finishing breakfast on the morning in question, 12-year-old Gordie sat entranced over his father's copy of *The Montreal Gazette*, feverishly devouring the description of the first ever organized ice hockey game played just last night in Victoria Skating Rink. Although only 40 spectators had witnessed the match, Gordon saw the game so vividly in his imagination that he felt he was one of them. The excitement of the new sport stayed with the boy as his parents packed the family into the horsecar, growing all throughout the ride to the far edges of Vieux-Montréal to visit his father's father. Gordon simply could not believe his eyes when upon walking into the new sitting room, already full of various aunts, uncles, and older cousins, his vision came to rest upon a portrait of a frozen lake in the mists of a wintry day where a small crowd had gathered around four men in top hats and brightly colored tweeds standing about with long sticks, one of them majestically hovering over a ball and taking aim at a stake positioned further down the pond. Gordon stood staring in amazement. This was not Victoria Rink, he knew, having skated there many a time. Nor was it the game he had read about in the morning paper, though there were striking similarities. How could such a thing exist? Despite his mother's protestations, Gordie would not sit down, as all available chairs faced away from this wonder.

His grandfather came and placed a kindly hand on Gordon's shoulder. "That, my boy, is the magnificent game of kolf. We used to play it in the old country. Well, the old old country, when I would visit *my* opa in Hollande. And this scene depicting its splendor was painted by none other than the Dutch master himself, Raymond Kolk!"

Gordie looked up excitedly. "Pépère, did you see the newspaper this morning?"

"I did indeed. What those boys are doing is a little different than what we've got here." Then, leaning down to face Gordon at eye level, exclaimed, "And say, what do we have *here*? On your upper lip?" Pépère Mathieu broke into a wide smile, rustling the boy's hair as he led him to two nearby seats and turned them towards the object of their admiration.

This comment was not lost upon Gordon Mathieu as he sat with his grandfather, who explained this other new, or rather centuries-old, game that he had never heard of before today. Kolf. Hitting a ball with sticks and clubs, across fields, through towns, and, yes, sometimes over frozen lakes. The target being, not a wide physical goal like in hockey, but rather a much smaller hole to drop the ball in, or stake to strike against. Gordie could tell this painting was special to his grandfather by the tender look in his eye as he spoke, and the fact that it was placed at the very center of the wall, all the other artwork emanating out in concentric circles from its focal point. His grandfather's words calling attention to his newfound peach fuzz seemed to echo down the centuries, materializing in full glory on the facial features of the most prominent figure in the painting. Gordie could not help but be mesmerized by this commanding presence standing front and center in supreme concentration over his ball, and by the fact that from this august personage's own lips drooped a mighty moustache, falling well below shoulder length and appearing to intertwine with his stick. Gordie began to sense that this vision might actually have been his grandfather in another time, and would have come to believe so had not Pépère Mathieu just then relayed the title and date of the Kolk they were gazing at—'Joost de Heer The Elder Contemplates His Opening Shot, 1695'. Although he hadn't the psychoanalytical terminology for it at the time, Gordon was aware of a great gathering of forces, that what was happening on this momentous day—with the news of last night's game, the fact that his own body hair had only just begun to sprout a week earlier, and now this exhilarating canvas—all these were somehow related. Key components in what he later came to regard as 'The Great Synchronicity of March 4, 1875'. And Gordon Mathieu never forgot his grandfather's words to him right before the two were called back into the family conversation. "I'm glad you appreciate it, my boy. This painting is one of my most prized possessions. And it has always been a dream of mine to own another Kolk."

Ice hockey began to take off, if not like wildfire, which would of course melt the area of play, then by at least its polar equivalent in force. Gordie became proficient at the game rather quickly. He could already skate well, and thus concentrated on handling his stick, all the while keeping a strong image of what he would become burning bright in his mind. There are times when writing itself can be a magical act, the mechanics of spelling things out, as it were, and just such an opportunity came in the week leading up to Christmas when a class assignment asked the pupils to outline what they wanted to do when they left school. Gordie feverishly set to work, the figure of Joost de Heer The Elder blazing in front of him as pencil danced across page, describing his champion hockey player status and how his extensive moustache would wrap around his stick to give more power to his play. The essay ending with a dazzling evocation of the final minutes of his most famous match, stealing the puck deep in his own zone to charge like lightning up the ice, defenders spinning dizzily behind in his wake. With moustache twirled about his trusty twig, head optimally bent over, the new center of gravity giving him that much more torque, he fakes to his right and lets rip a thunderous backhander with only three seconds left on the clock. Sailing clear past a goalie who never saw it coming. The crowd erupts as Mathieu is crowned scoring champion for the fifth year running.

For young Gordon and his friends, in the days when the game was new and no one could foresee what techniques its future leaders might possess, the notion of such hair winding down one's lumber like a serpent on the caduceus of Mercury didn't seem so outlandish. Miss Shields, however, whose surname perhaps caused her to feel a touch too much sympathy for said goalie, didn't see things the same way. He received the essay back after the holidays, a red pen remarking 'Your moustache will be tied around your stick? You'll shoot your eye out, kid!"

But nothing could deter Gordie's dream. He left school the next year at age 13, it having become almost impossible to get him off the ice and into a classroom anyway. But he was nothing if not enterprising, and earned his living carving hockey sticks, mending skates, and—as he continued to grow out and lovingly tend to his hair, picking up the finer points of style, shape, and what it means to be well-groomed—manufacturing what he called Haircare And Brush Sets (HABS) which he would sell at games, rinks, and occasionally door to door. As the amateur hockey clubs began to form, Mathieu was much sought after throughout Montreal and beyond, with the Saint-Laurent Stingrays finally snatching him up. It has many times been called into question how 'amateur' the league was in regards to players receiving payment, but this didn't stop Gordie from continuing to sell his HABS and perform a wide variety of trick shots for touring circus companies in between hockey matches. He was also generous with his time and money, teaching children to skate and shoot, and donating equipment to various youth organizations. There was one thing he kept secretive, of course. Despite many other players attempting to attach their own boisterous moustaches to their lumber, Gordie never let on just what it was that made his own combination so effective.

In 1883, the same year the extended family would be gathering in Vieux-Montréal for his grandfather's 60th birthday celebrations, Gordon was invited to take part in an international exhibition match, playing left wing for Canada against The Netherlands in Amsterdam. The voyage was eye-opening for Gordie, the ocean air wreaking havoc with his finely-tuned facial locks, the salt content not only drying them out but also adding curls against the natural warp, all proving suboptimal when translated to his stick-handling. Over the course of the ten days at sea, whenever the team wasn't training, he was scouring the ship for any unguents that might help him regain some sort of control. The ladies onboard were only too happy to help such a uniquely talented young man, rapturously wrapping his hair around their fingers as they applied luxurious creams and emollients. And how could he not repay them with demonstrations of what his mouth mane could do? But they had only brought so much with them, and demand far outweighed their supplies.

Upon disembarking, Gordie set out immediately to roam the city in search of the exotic argan, jojoba, and hemp oils of which the ship's medical staff had told tale. Bustling through the Leidseplein, he soon turned onto the Kerkstraat and stopped dead in his tracks. Could it be? Beaming from the window of a certain Kousemaker Gallery? Surely the brush strokes bore the distinctive style of none other than Raymond Kolk! Mathieu rushed into the shop to inquire and the kindly man behind the desk smiled and held up a forefinger, asking him to wait. In a minute he reemerged from the back of the shop carrying two further portraits. Gordie could scarcely believe it when the second frame was uncovered, reuniting him with a vision he knew so well. Joost de Heer The Elder once again stood before his eyes, this time hovering over a young boy, the dapper gentleman letting his moustache droop down onto the stick he's teaching the child to use. The gallery proprietor beamed, " 'Joost de Heer The Third Takes His First Swing'." A price was negotiated, still far beyond what Mathieu had on his person or had even brought with him on this trip. He made a small down payment, keeping enough back to buy oils and hair tonics, for he would need his moustache in tiptop shape if he were to continue to bring in any money playing hockey. Clutching the receipt in his hand, he raced back to the hotel where the team were staying. As luck would have it, they were still checking in, allowing Gordie to corner the team manager and ask to be remitted the money for his room. The manager reluctantly agreed, believing such moustache upkeep had gotten way out of control, but kept his views to himself, reckoning they'd need Mathieu to win the match. Now holding half of the required funds, as Gordie set out scouting for a bench to spend his nights upon, he caught sight of a pond complete with goal posts. Upturning his hat onto the ground, he laced up skates, wound tasche around stick, and began performing trick shots to the delight of passersby. Children were soon pushing produce out onto the ice to see what he would do with it. Tomatoes, potatoes, gourds of all sizes, and his particular favorite, heads of lettuce. He could time it just right to have an apple and an onion, shot one right after the other, meet simultaneously at an awaiting goalpost, to be crowned a split second later by a head of iceberg. At the end of the afternoon his hat was full of coin, almost the amount of cash to match the number on his receipt. The next morning he called for a private meeting with the team treasurer and managed to obtain an advance on his part of the prize money Canada would receive for winning the match. With such a deal in place, there was no choice but to succeed.

In the short time he had before dinner, Gordie strode confidently back to Kousemaker's, suffused with a warm feeling of pride that he would be giving his grandfather such a gift for his 60th birthday. As the proprietor handed over the painting, wrapped in brown paper and string, a thought occurred to Gordon. Sleeping in parks as he was, the weather was as much an issue as everything else. Where would he store this precious mural? After hearing Gordie's predicament, Kousemaker agreed to hold onto it for him, finding it curious that the Canadians would travel so far and not book anywhere to stay.

The game was a scorcher. The crowd, overenthusiastic from the beginning, had to be repeatedly told to calm down. It was the children who were the most excitable, more interested in seeing Gordie hack at fruit, which they had brought plenty of to throw on the ice, than the hockey itself. After Gordie racked up a hat trick 20 minutes in, amidst the cascade of projectiles being catapulted into the rink, he addressed the crowd, asking them to please refrain from such activity until after the game, when he would kindly oblige any vegetable they felt needed attending to. At the end of regulation time the score was 9-9. Gordie's body ached from sleeping on cold park benches and using money he might have spent on food for hair ointments, but it must be said, he was playing the best hockey of his life. His moustache, however, had been playing up all game. The copious lubricants required to combat the adverse effects of the sea air had not all washed out when it came time to tie his tasche to his twig and, despite his best efforts, kept slipping from its knots. He did his best to hide and covertly correct this during regulation play. After all, his stick/face combo was partly what the crowds had come to see. But then ten minutes into overtime, rushing up the ice, he received a pass from Combes on the inside of his blade. Spinning round for a backhanded shot, his right braid became completely disentangled, hanging there on its own as Gordie, lumber, and puck all twirled in the opposite direction. His head still attached by the left side of his tasche, the free righthand locks now gave the impression of a second stick, one that was also taking a shot on goal. The Netherlands tender didn't know which way to look as Gordie pounded in the biscuit to win it for Canada. The arena went wild. As promised, Gordie stayed late into the night, netting fruits, vegetables, and assorted other biological matter much to the delight of the crowd. His team left long before he did, the manager declaring there would be a bed waiting for him at the hotel that evening.

Bright and early the following morning, Kousemaker met Gordie at the port customs house, congratulating him on a game most excellently played. As the team would no doubt be celebrating the entire voyage home, now extended to pick up passengers from St. Andrews and Aberdeen, Scotland, Gordie asked the porter if the portrait might be stored somewhere away from such revelry. Before handing it over for safe keeping, he loosened its wrappings to once again spy his true accomplishment of this transatlantic voyage. His grandfather was going to be thrilled. Waving goodbye to Kousemaker and the gathering of fans who had assembled, Gordie picked up his extra valise full of balms, salves, and lotions and boarded the vessel.

After leaving Scotland, the waters turned turbulent, and the team's festivities, while not curtailed, were increasingly punctuated by rushes to the rails, expelling what they had just imbibed. More surefooted merrymaking awaited the team with gala receptions planned in the ports of Halifax, Quebec City, and, of course, Montreal. Gordie knew it was his duty to attend all these but he was itching to grab his luggage and press on to see his family. His grandfather's birthday was less than a week away. There was, however, a problem.

When finally the speeches had all been given and the toasts had all been drunk, when his teammates were all collapsing into various strange beds all about the city, Gordon stood again on a quayside awaiting delivery of his precious package. It was not forthcoming. The steward was most apologetic, even taking the nervous young man back into the hold to have him see the large empty space for himself. Because this was Gordon Mathieu, who had just brought Canada such international glory, the captain was alerted, and that venerable navigator issued an all-out search of the ship, assuring the star they would do their utmost to retrieve his cargo. Gordon even called the police and a trio of officers arrived to handle the case, standing close together, jotting down details as the Sun sank past visibility, making way for a long night into which the young hero eventually headed home.

Gordie was dejected. His family's congratulatory exuberance brought him little cheer as he confessed the fate of his grandfather's gift. Pépère Mathieu, whose own proud upper lip was now also in full bloom, shared Gordie's sorrow but was of course touched by the enormous gesture his grandson had wrought. Gordie did his best to not bring down the birthday celebrations but retired early, claiming he was still feeling the effects of the voyage. He was not to be seen for several days afterwards, this being due to the fact that he hadn't left his bed. He spent considerable time debating whether or not he should hang up his skates. Hockey, inexplicably, had brought a great deal of darkness into his life, when once it had seemed such a source of joy. Besides, having learned even more about hair care aboard ship, his HABS business would flourish. But depression, as it often does, continued to drag him down. After several weeks of isolation, his family carried him off to the local hospital.

After a thorough examination, the psychiatric ward officials conferred in a corner, eyes darting back and forth to Gordie, their fingers making scissor motions. The man presumed to be in charge stepped away from the group, cleared his throat, and pulled a long sharp razor from his pocket. "I'm afraid we'll have to shave off that moustache of yours lest you do anything stupid with it."

The doctor moved towards him. Panicked, Gordie looked to his grandfather, who once again, and especially now with such a bounteous tasche himself, merged with the vision of Joost de Heer The Elder, first seen all those years ago and sending him on this journey across seas and borders and many a patch of ice. Gordie jumped from the observation table, body checking the doctors out of the way, and raced straight to the rink. Who was he to deny Canadian audiences the chance to see the legendary moustache deke on their home soil?

Pépère Mathieu smiled and thanked the attendants, who were anyways not too bruised. Their own fake-out had worked as planned.

Face Hit

Barry Bajusz, known to one and all as 'BB Gun' due to his rifle-like throwing arm, was one day in late October of 1953, in a most peculiar twist of irony, using this very item. The season had ended early for the Maple Heights Magyars, the Ohio League baseball team situated in this heavily Hungarian suburb of Cleveland, with their having failed to make the play-offs for the second year running. It was a pleasant afternoon, however, throughout which Barry and fellow Magyar Philip 'YaYa' Gabor had been lining up their many emptied beer cans on top of the fence in Barry's backyard and picking them off with said pistol. Although Barry would claim the drink made him a better shot, and this seemed to be indisputable on the field, the accumulation of lager in his bloodstream and the sound of a neighbor's hound rushing through his huckleberry bushes combined to throw him off. Almost imperceptibly the pellet went wide of the can, those millimeters enough to send it flying into the Flanders' open second story window behind them. The two drunkenly gaped at the shadowy rectangle, only to be taken aback when Edwina Flanders calmly and coldly strolled out the door one level below heading straight towards them. She was wearing a large red wig, wielding a ruby scepter, and, in her other hand, brandishing a book, or what remained of one. "Gentlemen," she began, "I was just trying on my Halloween costume, when what should sail in through my window and lodge itself into *Through The Looking-Glass*? Luckily it was propped open on my dresser. I mean really, you could have broken *my* mirror!" Shoving the pages at Barry, who saw that the object on its cover had not escaped such a fate, she demanded, "You will replace my copy post-haste, Mr. Bajusz, and remember it's *Through The Looking-Glass*, the second one, not *Alice's Adventures In Wonderland*." With a regal sweep, she turned around and proceeded back into her home. Moments later there was an audible thud as the window came protectively down.

YaYa exhaled what seemed to be a sigh of relief. "Good thing you missed that mirror. We don't need any more bad luck," wiping his brow on his hairy hand before cracking open another beer.

But Barry wasn't so sure. A peculiar chill had swept through him when Edwina handed over the text and he saw the fate of Alice's famous looking-glass. He was a man prone to pondering, and now wondered aloud "What happens when you break an image of a mirror? Does it still count? And the damage appeared in an actual one! So is that double the bad luck?"

YaYa did not attempt to hide his confusion. "What are you talking about?"

"Well," Barry considered. "Mrs. Flanders was trying on a costume in the mirror, right? And she had that book propped open on her dresser so she could check her outfit, correct?"

YaYa nodded noncommittally.

"Well then, when the bb hit the book, destroying its cover and the mirror on its cover, this would have been reflected in *her* mirror, doubling the damage. Now, I didn't technically break a mirror, but still there's evidence which shows a broken mirror. So it could be nothing. It could be mediated to something like three and a half years, it could stand at seven, or it could be fourteen. This one's a pickle."

YaYa's eyes opened hungrily. "Let's go get some pickles!"

Barely had they cracked open the jar in the kitchen than the phone rang. Barry answered with some apprehension. He had a bad feeling about this, and was proved right when the Magyars manager informed him that next season the team would be moving to Garfield Heights and changing its name to the Goulash. After replacing the receiver, Barry was speechless for a moment before relaying the news to YaYa.

"Let's go get some goulash!" the latter enthusiastically responded.

As Barry approached his vehicle, he tripped on a stone, falling face first into the car door. Was Miss Fortune at work already? If she was, YaYa was too busy laughing to notice as he hopped in the passenger side. But as Barry backed out onto the street, he narrowly missed another hound rushing across his driveway. After a moment's consideration, he parked the car in front of his house and announced they were walking, which was a wise idea, given their advanced states of inebriation.

Once inside the cool, dark interior of Lugosi's, which may or may not have been decorated for the upcoming Halloween, it was always hard to tell, Barry began to feel calmer, a sense of peace descending through all the spice in the air. The goulash was the best in the city, and it was no less superb today as the two settled in to discussing the practical matters of moving the club all of two miles to Garfield Heights.

"Maybe we'll get more free food with the new name," YaYa offered cheerfully.

Just at this moment, halfway through his meal, Barry's dilated pupils froze as they took in what was sitting atop his heaping spoonful. An adhesive strip, the size of which you'd wrap around someone, say a chef's, finger and stained the color of his otherwise delicious goulash, making it impossible to tell if the bandage had already been used or not. Angling for even more complimentary courses, YaYa called over the owner, Arisztid, who apologized profusely, and began plying the two with hopefully enough Unicum and pálinka to make them forget the whole experience. On the house, of course. He was, after all, an avid baseball fan and appreciated their patronage. After the third round, Barry and YaYa invited this melancholy gentleman to join them and as the three got progressively more plastered, secrets began to be shared. YaYa letting slip about the team's move and in sympathy Arisztid commenced sobbing, eager to unload his own hidden darkness. He called Chef Tas out of the kitchen and commanded him to show the two customers his right forefinger. Barry and YaYa peered close until their breath froze, now staring at four tiny puncture holes, two up two down, swirling before their very eyes. "It was but a baby, a tiny little bat." Arisztid cutting in, "Do not worry, indeed have no fears whatsoever. Tas was driven straight to the emergency room where he was given a smorgasbord of jabs and pills for rabies, histoplasmosis, Weil's disease, and whatever else."

Despite Arisztid's reassurances and the copious amounts of alcohol consumed so far that day, a sense of unease began to permeate Barry's very being. Leaving their host weeping into the crook of his elbow on the table, Barry and YaYa exited the establishment and proceeded immediately to the hospital where the sympathetic staff remembered Tas' recent visit all too well. Barry would have his own series of shots but first he needed to sober up. He opted to pass out in a free bed on the second floor. No such luxury was offered YaYa, who, promising to check in on his friend tomorrow, hurried back to Lugosi's for hopefully more free beverages.

While Barry made his way home the next day, eyes all bloodshot, stomach dyspeptic, arm quite sore, feeling certainly worse for the wear and unable to recall the sight atop his spoon without having to stifle the reflex to retch, he considered himself fortunate that waking up in a hospital allowed him to receive swift medical attention. But as he then went over the events of the previous 24 hours, he wondered if he would actually call any of this 'lucky'. In fact, ever since he shot the hole in the mirror on that book cover, some pretty awful things had been happening to him. And by focusing on these, that barely planted seed of a bb pellet blossomed into dark alluring flowers begging Barry to stop and take them in, to believe in the curse their petals were offering. Captivated by the complexities of it all, next thing he knew he was on his street, his house already in sight with his car inexplicably sitting in front of it with—what's this?—a parking ticket for street cleaning attached to its windshield.

Barry arrived at spring training with a mile-long list of the misfortunes that had befallen him over the previous months.

His Halloween happened to be all trick and no treat with the neighborhood teenagers lighting his front lawn on fire, on Thanksgiving a dead mouse had been found in the turkey carcass, and Christmas Eve saw a bat, much larger than the one Tas had described, bolt down his chimney. On New Year's Day he woke up so hungover it was many hours before he could feel his teeth again. And the calamities weren't just reserved for the holidays. His body bore various bruises from humdrum everyday activities such as slicing his hand on the mailbox, supermarket doors slamming on his torso, even getting out of bed proved most precarious as bottles left on the floor provided the means to slip over and crack his head upon dresser drawer, window sill, or other beverage-bearing containers. All of which occurred repeatedly. Adding to this, the new name emblazoned on his uniform was a constant reminder of the incident at Lugosi's, prompting him to drink a great deal more to blackout the memory and inkling that, given another second or two, he very well may have chewed upon someone else's bandage that had been covering a bat bite. Barry continued, however, to patronize the restaurant with his teammates—they were indeed being given many a meal on the house thus turning this into a pre-game tradition—though he himself always stuck solely to beverages, which often moved him into sulky darker hours hyperfocused on Tas' incisors, sure that they had somehow grown sharper, and obsessing over the fact that the rooms seemed to contain no reflective surfaces.

And problems continued to arise. Barry was only hitting .230 while mysterious pains in his mouth necessitated multiple trips to the dentist. Nursing an icepack to his jaw after one such visit, he decided the best course of action was to attempt to counteract all this bad mojo, cut it off at the pass before it grew any worse. He needed a good luck charm, something he could carry on his person always. The trouble with something like a rabbit's foot or a bracelet or necklace was that he always seemed to be losing things these days. Since New Year's he had misplaced his wallet a whopping five times, each instance taking days to recover, once finding it in YaYa's refrigerator, another under the front left wheel of his car. Barry now stood before his bathroom mirror, fervently hoping he mightn't inadvertently call on any spirits of the nether world who would conspire to break it on his behalf, and gazed thoughtfully at his image. After some moments it hit him and he nodded slowly in approval. Although they hadn't been seen in the world of baseball much since 1914, the moral code of the country dictating that those who would professionally pursue its national pastime be clean-cut, Barry knew of many a man of action around the world who considered rubbing their moustache to be an act of *good* luck. The more he thought about it, the more this seemed the perfect solution. Facial hair could be seen in a mirror, somehow placating looking-glasses everywhere for that first offense, and a moustache was something he couldn't *not* carry with him at all times. There and then he set about growing one, even watching himself in the glass for a further quarter of an hour, though espying no discernible darkening in the area betwixt nose and lip.

As the hairs began to grow, at first nothing much changed. Coach Kis, who in keeping with the conservative customs of recent decades likened the act to putting on make-up, but he could also see that Barry had a black cloud hanging above his head, one full of albatrosses who were constantly pecking at the poor man whilst taking turns defecating upon his shoulders. He listened to Barry's reasoning and reluctantly gave the moustache a probationary period. Perhaps the biggest difference came from the phasing out of his being known as 'BB Gun', a fortunate development as the epithet persistently reminded Barry of why he was in this mess in the first place. Bajusz, like many family names that came over from Europe around the turn of the 20th century, had quickly become anglicized, if not fully Americanized, simply through the insistence on sight rather than sound. W's widened into wings from their initial V-like sharpness, while J's everywhere were twisted from their soft pretzel-esque Y pronunciation into the firmer baton of the sound as we know it. And so Bajusz, halfway there already, rolled quite naturally with the changes on his upper lip to denote both player and tasche as 'Ba Juice Strainer', teammates soon dropping the 'ba' without any sheepishness at all. This brought Barry great relief, for although 'goulash', being itself a kind of soup, might have easily been bestowed upon any moustache appearing on the field, the constant calls of that nickname would have been too great a strain on his nerves, positioning his mouth and Lugosi's specialty close enough together to imply the swallowing of a used bandage.

As the season proper began, it was hard to tell if Barry's luck was lightening at all. Styling his new charm for opening day, he had used enough wax to temporarily blind himself as sunbeams reflected off at odd angles in the top of the second inning, causing him to miss an easy catch that allowed two runs to score. He had a deuce of a time convincing Coach Kis, who was holding up a razor upon his return to the dugout, to let the hair even stay in the game. Incredibly, this was to happen twice again—three days later and once more the following week. After this latest mishap, which even so saw the Goulash win 5-2, Coach Kis told Barry "You got to choose. Either that thing on your lip or your baseball career." The decision seemed obvious, though with the next day off, Barry delayed shaving until the last possible moment. At 8 p.m. that night, just as he had gotten drunk enough to lather up, the doorbell rang. An apologetic coach stood cap in hand. He was still against the moustache to be sure but he knew his rulings should be authentic. As it happens, the wax wasn't responsible for any errors after all. Stadium security had taken into custody one Teddyboy Flanders, husband of Edwina, who had been caught in the stands with a compact mirror directing the Sun into Barry's eyes. While himself a Magyars then Goulash fan, Flanders had found the act of Barry giving his wife a book to be highly suspicious and was thus seeking revenge. Kis concluded, "It's alright. You can keep furry friend. For now."

After the coach had left, Barry collapsed into his armchair delighted, cracking open a celebratory beer. He had grown quite fond of the hair and intended to ride its charms for all they were worth. For there was certainly some effect. He no longer tripped as often when he walked, his batting average was up to .280, and he had even been able to accept a plate of Töltött Káposzta at Lugosi's the other night. He was no longer 'Bad News Barry'.

The effect of Cleveland's major league team doing so well this 1954 season was two-fold for the Goulash. Caught as the population was in the grips of baseball fever, fans were getting all they could take on any field found across the city and its outskirts. Secondly, success caused the authorities to look the other way regarding Barry's flourishing fuzz. Sure there were many who considered it a personal affront to their patriotism, as well as those who decried the moustache as the décor of the dictator. But there were also legions of fans who believed in its good luck properties as Barry did. And who knew, perhaps the hair even radiated its own prosperity over the greater metropolitan area. Barry was soon hitting .333, a statistic that—if you tilt your head to the right—looks very much like triple moustaches lined up on top of each other, all hung over the end of a bat pointing towards the bleachers for a homer. To celebrate, the stadium even began selling 'Ba Juice', heralded as a non-alcoholic palinka to be enjoyed by all ages, but in reality just a lightly carbonated apple-flavored drink.

The minor league season wrapped in September, a few weeks before the majors, with Garfield Heights its champions. Barry hitting three out-of-the-park home runs in the final, sweeping them in a wide arc—high over the left field fence in the first inning, then shooting dead center in the third, finally racing past the right bleachers in the eighth—and was awarded MVP. There were plenty of unofficial whispers too about a certain VPM—Very Powerful Moustache. With his confidence and clout riding high, on the last day of the month Barry marched into the head office to discuss switching the name back to the Magyars, unhappy as all the players were—the team being of mostly Hungarian descent—with 'Goulash'. Barry even offered to, if the change was accepted, fashion his tasche into a giant M, which would surely drive the fans wild. He was told top brass would mull it over, before being quickly shown the door. But the mood changed in the city that week as Cleveland were swept by New York in the World Series and, far from winning them over to his cause, Barry's proposal brought the club owners' attention to his, until then flying under the radar, facial hair.

Although the atmosphere about the city was dour, Barry did not let this diminish his own change in fortunes. What a difference a year makes. Dressed as the Walrus to YaYa's Carpenter, the two along with Mrs. Flanders, reprising her previous costume, set up beach chairs next to the cauldron of candy and half-keg of lager on Barry's front lawn, all the better to keep it from burning this year. The same could not be said of Edwina's husband who watched the trio with a pair of binoculars from the same window the bb had flown in one afternoon last October. Barry's anxiety over every meal served to him had greatly decreased, though he still stayed away from goulash or any dish that a bandage might camouflage itself within. And how nice it was to not have to chase a bat out of one's home whilst hungover in the early hours of Christmas morning.

But the nature of changing fortunes is just that. Coach Kis, who had come to believe in the power of the tasche, allowed Barry to keep it through the new year and all of spring training, despite word coming early from Goulash management that shaved it must be. Things came to a head the evening before the first game of the new season, with owner William Ockham in particular putting his foot down about the whole business. He wasn't going to have a team of radical Communists intent on overthrowing the league. Kis reminded him that it was largely due to Barry's prowess that the Goulash were the current champions, though so prevalent was anti-moustache sentiment that a good percentage of upper management, as well as certain fans, believed that Barry's facial hair might have loaded his own bases at the expense of the rest of the city's blessings. Coach Kis bargained to allow Barry one last game with the tasche, the opening match-up of the season against the Cincinnati Gnatwings. This was agreed upon, and although he couldn't speak in an official capacity, in an effort to pack the stands, Coach Kis let it slip that this would be the fans' last chance to see The Juice Strainer in action.

After doing so, Kis made his way to Barry's house to break the news, finding Barry and YaYa once again drinking from a half-keg on the front lawn, a pastime they had taken to whenever the weather called for it. Barry listened stoically. His moustache, it seemed, had also brought him wisdom. For as he stroked its magnificent bristles, he realized that this must be so, and resolved to put on a good show for the fans one last time. He made the decision not to indulge in his usual pre-game wax, instead letting the hairs flow wild, to dance in celebration of themselves and their greater communal structure.

Coach Kis, along with most everybody else, still referred to The Goulash's upcoming rivals as 'The Gnats', as the Cincinnati club had been known up until two years previous when they opted to follow the lead of their major league seniors who had amended their own name to 'Redlegs' in order to distance themselves from any communist connotations. The Gnats soon following suit, though without any clear idea how anyone could link an innocent Midwestern insect with Stalin and Khrushchev.

Coming to the plate in the bottom of the first with two men on base and one out, Barry grabbed his lucky slugger and was greeted with thunderous applause as he stepped out of the dugout. He lifted his head to the heavens to allow the stands a view of the soon-to-be-departed strands. The stadium shook with wild abandon as devoted fans let whoop and roar from the depths of their beings. Barry took his time, soaking it all in, even going so far as to linger over the batter's box sketching a moustache in the dirt—two angel wings on which he hoped both hit and hair would be delivered into the glorious after-lives awaiting them. He stared hard at the owners' box as he stepped up to the plate, digging his heel symbolically into this likeness. And homered for three.

So far the game was proving to be a fitting send-off for his tasche, and at his next at bat Barry opted to have a little fun. The second pitch was inside, so Barry jumped out of the way screaming in mock pain, claiming the ball had hit The Juice Strainer itself and that he deserved to head to first. Umpire Stanley Witz, however, was having none of it. Barry smiled and doubled, sending YaYa home from third. And despite the Gnatwings tying it up in the eighth at 7-7, with the much-loved moustache having only precious few more minutes on Barry's upper lip, his mischievous mood continued.

Bottom of the ninth with the score still tied. Barry on third with two outs. He's never been quite so audacious before but why not? and begins to edge himself off the bag. Cincinnati pitcher Joseph Koba winds up and just as the ball leaves his fingertips, Barry's booking it down the baseline. Catcher Walter Ulya barely has time to register what's happening as Barry's sliding face first into home plate. His arms go wide as the dust clouds leap into the air around him, Ulya jumping back into position, reaching down to tag his adversary. Umpire Witz is peering through the veil of dirt hanging between him and the players, fist primed to call Barry out and extend the game into extra innings. But just before Witz heaves his hand skywards, Ulya reflexively grinds his right foot and Witz sees Barry grimace. The umpire lifting Ulya's leg to reveal Barry's moustache flopped forward onto the plate, underneath Ulya's cleet. "Safe!" And the Goulash win it 8-7. The crowd erupts and Barry is carried off the field in triumph, spotlights illuminating the VPM. Celebrations of the soon-to-be-famous "not even by a nose, by a moustache" play continue long into the next morning, the scene at Lugosi's just past 9 a.m. being one of pure carnage.

Even with the legendary victory, management still insisted Barry shave. Fresh-faced, he played fine over the course of the season, though of course there was the psychological toll, especially as his batting average dropped to .295, the tasche-like 3's vanishing as well. The Goulash made the playoffs but did not progress far. And the same continued for the lifespan of the club, who retained their name through their final season much to the disgruntlement of the players. There have been many curses that came to beleaguer Cleveland's sports teams over the years, with proponents of quite a few of them claiming collective responsibility for the whole city. Just like those, anyone who was there the night Barry stole home will tell you The Curse of The Ba Juice Strainer is the real deal.

8

First & Mane

COMING FROM a town with such a name, one might feel a kinship with outer space, may even be viewed as a bit of an oddball, and the same was no different for Coach Jason Jaspers of Jupiter College's Fighting Jackrabbits. From an early age, Jaspers dressed in nonsensical colors and pattern combinations, affected smoking a pipe made from imitation ivory which he did not light or inhale, often feigning to forget it was hanging from his mouth though it kept a 45 degree angle out the left corner with almost military precision, and was an aficionado of avant-garde jazz and classical music, frequently manipulating the answer to a simple 'how are you?' through long digressions detailing his hopes of a merger between the two seemingly disparate compositional styles. His first year as coach, Jaspers would claim to have devised football plays based on the recent newspaper reports he'd read of the riots at the premiere of Stravinsky's 'The Rite Of Spring' that summer of 1913, strategies which no one bothered to question as long as they were effective, and he would later come to adore the music of Sun Ra, who himself claimed to be from Saturn. Jaspers could go one further, his birth certificate proving he was born right there in The Sunshine State's own town of Jupiter. Jaspers was also the best coach that area of Florida had ever seen. Nearly undefeated, the only ones keeping him from that claim were archrivals The Torts, who hailed from the highly suspicious, even right down to its name, US Legal, an unaccredited school whose home field, if not amorphous campus, was an hour's drive from Jupiter. The so-called 'university' 's sole qualification for teaching law seemed to be their construction of a labyrinthine charter so complex that fans of their athletic department dare not question it.

Jupiter is said to be the planet of benevolence, producing leaders under the sign of Leo. Of course Jaspers had his Moon and Ascendant in Aquarius, which often accounts for eccentricity. But Coach Jaspers didn't have much time for astrology, he had football games to win. His style of dress could be traced to him just throwing on whatever clothing item was found nearest his bed in the morning. If one looked closely enough they would notice deep teeth marks on the ivory pipe's mouthpiece, a substitute for the cigarettes Jaspers would not smoke, setting an example for his team who needed all their lungpower to be the fastest in their division. And his love of those peculiar horn lines or the erratic vibrato on a particular violin passage stemmed from using these as springboards, allowing his mind to cultivate ever more unexpected plays, formations which were then scribbled down on the cocktail napkins of underground nightclubs all over the South. His strategies were seen as so strange at times that others believed he actually was taking directions from the cosmos. But you can't argue with results, and you certainly wouldn't want to argue with Jaspers.

An imposing man, at a bulky six foot three with enormous ears and flopping feet, his prominent feature still managed to be his facial hair, a sort of moustache/goatee combo that there isn't readily a name for. Being as it was shaped like a J around his mouth. Straight moustache across upper lip, then connecting down the right hand side to curl under his chin and back up slightly, completing a little half-loop on the left, punctuated by the unlit pipe. It gave a sense of self, and served to remind people who they were speaking to, as the J was styled to face the public.

When at work, which was almost always, Jaspers' conspicuous clothes were covered by the lapis blue and caramel school jacket depicting their own Jack the Jackrabbit on the back. Slightly hairier than your average hare, with giant ears and long strong feet, your casual onlooker could not be faulted for guessing that Jaspers himself had posed as the model for this mascot. The truth is spookier. The artist had placed his design on the Athletic Director's desk not twenty minutes before Jaspers walked in to apply for the coaching job. Despite what he wore underneath said jacket, Coach Jaspers nevertheless demanded his team also present themselves accordingly when at work on the field. And part of the uniform was facial hair. Not just any moustache or beard either. Each position had its own specific style, something that reflected the nature of its role in the greater context of the line-up. But as one's whiskers are such a highly personal growth, almost a talisman of sorts, Jaspers encouraged his players to put their own individual spin on that spot. By the mid-1930's, young athletes in the area hoping to one day attend Jupiter College would often choose where in the lineup they wanted to be based on the beards they most admired.

To illustrate these fashions, let us take a look at the Fighting Jackrabbits roster going into the autumn 1938 season. Fullback Allan Keenan sported a full beard, going, as it did, all the way to the rear. Halfback Elliot Daniels featured a sort of extended goatee, not receding into the full distance though pushing the boundaries of strictly fifty-fifty, and with the corners sharpened to highlight his ability to pivot. Ends traditionally deployed bulging mutton chops and those featured on the faces of Lee Geddes and Neil Lifeson were no different. Wide receivers Randy Osbourne and Alan Morissette adopted the time-honored tactic of shaving oblong shapes into their beards, ready spaces for the ball to fall into. Quarterback Tom Reed displayed the toothbrush moustache, known then as the Charlie Chaplin, the style in his case metaphorically showing the ball as a tiny patch of hair sailing over the field of the lips. Defending Reed this year were Greg Williams, Peter Knight, and Bobby Lande, whose roles as linemen were seen in the bars of hair extended straight out from their philtrums in both directions. Coach Jaspers always spurred on new recruits to grow these as broad as possible, to stretch them out as far as they could reach, with the above trio certainly testing the limits of gravity this summer.

As curious as the conjunction of the Jackrabbit mascot blueprint arriving and Coach Jaspers' hiring, during tryouts for the upcoming season, onto the field walked one Helmut Zweck, freshman. His name was taboo, especially as rumors were heavily circulating that this was to be the final season before headgear would be required in college ball. But he shared with Jaspers the immovable belief that one's hair should suffice as one's helmet, and of his own he had fashioned those mutton chops worn by the Fighting Jackrabbits' ends into thick strips of lightning descending down his cheeks, guarding a football shape etched front and center into his chin. As he discussed his convictions regarding regulation equipment with Coach Jaspers, it was readily apparent that he would make the team, but what really clinched the deal was his explanation that lightning represented the speed that he travelled as both tight end and on the defensive line. "Where my family comes from, these . . ." Helmut craned his neck skyward, pointing proudly to the strokes, "are known as 'blitz'." Jaspers nodded, he liked the sound of this.

Coach encouraged his team to show off their beards and moustaches, believing them an integral part of each player's personality, radiant glories that this new helmet rule sought to dim. Already the headgear that was in play at some of the less fashion-conscious schools went over the ears by a good margin, rendering invisible most if not all of each highly cultivated, and highly adored, sideburn. It was here too that Jaspers seemed tuned into outer space, able to sense the future, for he could often be heard declaring that once the coverings began, it would only be a matter of time before more protection would mask their very mouths and all that sprouted around them. Jaspers, whose own head went to some faraway places, couldn't quite bring himself to believe the reasons helmets were becoming mandatory. The safety of his squad was important, yes, but blocking their faces and the totems he felt ensured the team's success was a cost almost too great to bear. He was essentially an honest man who believed all you needed to know about an athlete could be read in their facial hair. Oh what darkness would come into play when this would be obscured. He also regarded the seconds after the final whistle blew to be among the most inspirational scenes one could take in anywhere, whether by youths who fantasize of one day being on the field themselves, ex-cons trying to set speedboat jumping records in a remote bayou, or bootleggers transporting ever more ludicrous amounts of alcohol from Texas to Georgia, all could find the necessary motivation in the sunlight beaming off these regal sweat-soaked hairstyles straight into the eyes of the crowd. They bestowed upon everyone the power to make their own dreams come true. For over a decade now, years before Aleister Crowley would claim to have passed the symbol on to British Military Intelligence, Jaspers had pushed this golden moment further by having his team shape their post-game tasches into V's for Victory. This being easiest for kicker Vinny Ventura whose own strands stopped just short of his corneas, already waxed out and up into the two vertical bars of a goal post. Jaspers wasn't head coach for nothing.

By the start of the season proper, word had officially come down that this would be the last year bare play was allowed in the league, and Jaspers intended to make the most of it. Fans were encouraged to attend with their own stubble styled to match that of their favorite player. For those who could not grow enough facial hair, fake fur was sold at the concession stands. All the proceeds, like the moustaches themselves, went towards the glory of the team. An extra bus was hired to carry such costumed fans out to Port Marino for the first away game of the season. The PM Shadows coach, Rip Cordes, was outspoken about Jaspers' showmanship, though many felt this was poorly disguised jealousy considering the paltry size of the Port Marino home crowd. A good percentage of Shadows fans in attendance even forking out for Fighting Jackrabbits face wigs of their own, impressed with the rookie tight end's performance, but more by Helmut's girlfriend, Betty Hamilton, who led the boisterous cheerleading squad whilst sporting her beau's trademark lightning chops.

The Jackrabbits blew Port Marino out of the water, 48-3. Helmut Zweck playing like an aquatic bunny on fire. Leaping over fleets of opponents to catch twelve passes, including one in the endzone and another he ran 40 yards for a second touchdown, zigzagging and jumping over diving defenders all the way. On defense he sacked Shadows quarterback Cliff Marvin three times. The highlight of the game came late in the third quarter when Helmut picked up a Port Marino fumble and ran it back 80 yards to score again. He truly lived up to the lightning on his cheeks. And let's not forget Reed himself, who ran the ball for 75 yards, not so much because the Shadows defense warranted any scrambling but simply because he could.

As the season pressed on, The Jackrabbits were unstoppable. The connection between Reed and Zweck became almost telepathic, with Reed soon shaving the sides of his head into thunder cloud formations, firing the ball to Helmut wherever he was on the field. The quarterback was pleased as punch the first time someone referred to him as 'Thunder Reed', becoming blissful as an all-out brawl as further usage of this nickname spread.

Per usual, Jupiter College found itself facing US Legal in the final game of the season, and with both teams undefeated and playing so spectacularly, the winner would be going on to the Cannon Bowl that December in Winter Haven. While The Torts were sure to give Jaspers and co. a run for their money, Coach J played it cool in public, telling Jupiter's school newspaper, *The Read Spot*, that the game would be 'a piece of cake.' Privately he was less convinced. The Torts were universally hated, but they were a force to be reckoned with. Their green and brown uniforms, however, like camouflage, seemed to be hiding something. No one quite knew how they even qualified to be in the league. And as if to mock the Jackrabbits, The Torts had already been wearing helmets all season of their own accord. This confirmed Coach Jaspers' deepest beliefs, for the US Legal squad had no concern for common safety, and would regularly kick a player in the head after he was down. No, these outer shells of theirs were definitely concealing an interior most dark. The Torts' playing style was in line with what they taught at US Legal, long wars of attrition, seen in their short passing and running game, slowly gaining yardage up the field. Also like the school itself, their victories regularly had the ring of the criminal about them. Not a game went by without disputed calls, subterfuge, and acts of aggression that lingered just below what could be counted as a penalty. Since US Legal's inception ten years ago in 1928, The Jackrabbits and The Torts were an even 5-5 against each other, the new law school somehow managing to stay in business despite the country entering The Depression.

The morning before the big game, Tom Reed awoke in his car on the side of an unknown road with his tires deflated. He vaguely recalled being at a party the night before, down towards Boca Raton, and his hangover confirmed this. Glancing into his rearview mirror, his red eyes bulged as he let out a scream and then another one, this time tinged with vengeance. The patch of hair above his upper lip, the fuzz of the football, was gone. It was another moment before he noticed that one of his thunder clouds had been shaved off too. He might not be able to prove it in court, but he knew beyond a shadow of a doubt that this could only be the action of a Tort. He hitchhiked back to Jupiter and, with there being no easy way of breaking the news, went straight to the coach's office.

Jaspers was furious. Trashcans were kicked, lockers dented, oaths sworn to high heaven. US Legal would not get away with this. There was more riding on the game now than they ever could have imagined. Besides being possibly the last chance their beautiful facial locks might ever get to be on display, unencumbered by any sort of cover, a further score needed settling with their archrivals. Jaspers spent long hours alone in his office making impassioned telephone calls and wildly sketching new patterns into his playbook. He eventually emerged a much calmer man, possessed of an heroic confidence. When Coach Jaspers then sent his linemen to the local naval base for training, they did not question him. Nor did Reed when later that day, a wizened Chinese herbalist arrived at the field, himself possessing a magnificent knee-length white beard, and began to apply tinctures and lotions to Tom's upper lip, all hoping that the quarterback might be able to sprout back what he had lost overnight. The thunder clouds beneath his temples would be substituted with what was on sale at the concession stand, but Reed longed to flaunt at least some amount of authenticity during the big game. When he awoke the morning of the match, this time thankfully in his own bed, there was just the slightest bit more growth than two days stubble would suggest. Reed looked himself in the mirror and was ready.

From the opening kick-off, it was carnage. US Legal doing whatever they could to take out Helmut, who nonetheless managed to blaze over, under, and through their various attempts to trip, straight-arm, or flat-out punch him as he ran for more yardage. Tort linebackers Franklin and Keyes surrounded Zweck like electrons to his nucleus, doubleteaming him every play, whether he had the ball or not. But the violence wasn't only confined to the man with the lightning chops. Thrice, US Legal had to be warned about headbutting, even their own crowd booing the helmeted players who attempted to knock noses with their bareheaded opponents.

Halfway through the fourth quarter, it finally happened. With the score tied 28-28, Helmut caught a pass on The Torts 20 yard line as Franklin crashed into Zweck's upper body from the front while Keyes dove into the backs of his knees. The entire Torts team then piled on top. When the mess cleared, a mildly hallucinating Helmut insisted he would finish out the game despite not being able to move enough to kneel, let alone stand up. As he was carried out on a stretcher, Coach Jaspers focused his mind on what he had begun to put in motion the day before. Drunk on blood, with their next possession The Torts drove the ball up the Jackrabbits half, kicking a field goal at the 15 yard line to put them ahead by three. Helmut, refusing to leave the sidelines, sat touching the tips of his lightning bolts and staring out at his teammates with a gaze of such intensity no one dared walk in front of him lest they disturb whatever vibes he was sending out. With fifteen seconds left on the clock, Reed managed to get the ball to The

Torts two yard line before Jaspers called for a time-out. The moment had come to put his masterplan into action. Since this might very well be their moustaches' last play, it was going to be memorable. Arriving back at the line of scrimmage, Williams, Knight, and Lande applied what they had learned from yesterday's naval instructor, quickly tying the long bars of hair above their lips together to form an unassailable wall. The pigskin was snapped and, heads together, they dug in for their very lives. Constant groans of agony with facial expressions to match emanated from the men as they stood their ground. A brutal, difficult scene to witness, and yet it captured everything Coach Jaspers felt inside about the helmet regulations coming into play, the field holding a mirror to Jaspers' very soul. The trio somehow managed to stay on their feet and in front of Reed, who ran right looking for an open Osbourne or Morissette before switching back up left with Geddes and Lifeson moving in to block for him. Everything seemed to happen in slow-motion—the pangs of pain traversing the faces of Williams, Knight, and Lande, Helmut miraculously standing, still beaming positive energy to his teammates via his temples, and finally Reed barreling up the middle to dive up and over The Torts defensive line and into their end zone as the whistle blew. The Jackrabbits winning 34-31.

The crowd went wild, rushing down onto the field and lifting Reed aloft on jubilant shoulders. Jaspers ecstatically hoisting the rest of his team up too, intent on giving the moustaches their exultant due. It was some time before the bodies of Williams, Knight, and Lande were found unconscious on the ground, their faces still close to each other, deeply etched with wild contortions of pain. They were brought to the hospital along with Zweck. The following day US Legal issued a protest against Jupiter's linemen tying their hair together for the fateful play but before any decision could be reached, the ersatz law school would disappear overnight following accusations of racketeering.

Three weeks later Jupiter College went on to win The Cannon Bowl, 47–21, defeating the Hollywood Endings. It was a fine finale for the glorious facial hair of The Fighting Jackrabbits. Helmut Zweck, who missed the bowl game due to a broken tibia, recovered enough to distinguish himself over his next three years at JC, his prowess undiminished even when required to wear his namesake atop his head. Jaspers remained as head coach despite the game not meaning as much for him anymore. He would live to see his predictions about the totality of face masks come true, but by then he had moved to New York City, leaving the sport behind and spending most of his time immersed in the free jazz scene of the 1960's, himself taking up the jaleika. Still, he was proud of what he had accomplished as coach and of the many fine grooming styles with which his players had come to be known. Whenever he would hear Sun Ra, after some mindbending performance or other, claim to be from Saturn, Jaspers would smile and whisper to himself "And I'm from Jupiter."

Net Worth

HAILING AS HE DID from a long line of Georgia peach farmers, some of whose family's baskets no doubt ending up being nailed to balconies and poles as the game continued to further sweep the nation, Fate seemed to decree that the young Bartholomew Jordan's life would be tied up with the new sport of basketball then gaining popularity at the turn of the century. After an exceptionally easy birth in Augusta in 1888, which his mother would later describe as a 'swish', the hands of Destiny promptly pushed the Jordans further northwards. Bart's father—the fruitiers being on his mother's side—had obtained employment in the law firm of Dribble & Dribble, his wife and child joining him in Springfield, MA the winter of 1891, the very same season James Naismith's brain received an inbound pass from the ether and set about inventing what became known as 'basket ball' at Springfield College. The sport being such a local phenomenon, Bart was introduced to it at an early age and he was soon spending as much time on the court as his father did in his. When June came and his mother, per usual, took herself and son back down to Georgia to stay with her relatives, Bart insisted on bringing his ball, and was greeted by a Cubbins Family peach basket hanging atop a barn door which Uncle Theodor has installed for their arrival. "You read my mind!" Bart exclaimed, feeling a stirring of his own sense of Destiny. In reality, his mother had telegraphed ahead, but neither brother nor sister ever let on as the child practiced day and night. Despite his love of the game he had found there, always upon returning to Massachusetts after summering in the South, the young Herr Jordan would be more determined than ever to find a way to combat the bitter New England cold. As soon as the first peach fuzz poked through his chin, he commenced cultivating the facial hair for which he would become known, though initially it simply served as additional insulation against the winter's precipitous drop in temperature, not to mention its biting wind. Turns out he had a knack for this too, and by the age of 16 his blond beard was down to his collarbone.

At the beginning of his senior year of high school, refining both game and grooming, Bart shaved cheeks and neck, leaving a thick pipe of hair drooping far down past either side of his lips. Inspired, he took to waxing the ends. 'Bart's Darts' they called them, as he bent the locks a few inches above the nipple, refining each into a point. And of course began integrating these into play. Acting as an extra pair of hands, with a quick nod or shake of his head, such tips could jab the ball away from an unsuspecting opponent, leading to a steal and, more often than not, a successful run downcourt to the basket. After five games and many complaints, it taking this long for most teams to believe what they were seeing, such use of Bart's, or any, facial hair was banned from competition. The restriction was off the books of course, the Massachusetts Sports Teams Authority Council Headquarters (MSTACH) deciding not to institute an official ruling when circumstances as of yet only applied to one player. Unphased, Bart carried on, growing back his beard while his team went undefeated, winning their conference championships and a full scholarship for the hirsute Jordan.

Having been starting forward on every team since he had first picked up the ball, the position was fated for Bart when he enrolled as a freshman at Agawam College in 1906, making the cut for The Bats[1] varsity team that same year. He had always felt a special surge of pride when he walked out onto the court and saw the Cubbins Family logo stamped red on the awaiting baskets, his mother donating the copious containers that continually arrived on their doorstep from their Southern kin. But this was a bittersweet year for Bart—some would say just like his Aunt Georgina's rhubarb and peach pie—when the old fruit crates were replaced with metal rims and rope nets. Bart couldn't help but wonder, mourn a little even, if he was somehow losing his connection with the game. He needn't have worried for long.

At the end of the 1908-1909 season, during practice the night before the semi-final against the Southwick Candles, Jordan came crashing down from a lay-up and stared in utter surprise at the torn netting between his fingers. A glance up at the bare hoop confirmed what had just happened but Bart could scarcely believe his eyes—the net was not only off but ripped to shreds in his hands. Was this suppressed rage spewing forth? A turbulent unconscious kicking against the peach

[1]All Agawam sports teams took their names from the college's original baseball team.

baskets being rendered obsolete? It was only a few months ago that nets were cut at the bottom to allow the ball to pass through, and Jordan had remembered feeling some satisfaction at this, though how dark its origins he did not know. But Bart had been brought up to accept consequences and when Coach Day informed him that it was his responsibility to replace the net before tomorrow's game, Jordan resolved to doing just that. Having only 18 hours and without a clue where to procure such equipment soon proved more problematic. And besides, he had a post-practice date with the lovely Allison Cooper, who had been waiting patiently in the bleachers and caught the whole incident. The two made their way back to Jordan's lodgings for Bart to shower and change. This being 1909, Ms. Cooper was obliged to remain in the foyer. Post-ablutions, as Bartholomew stood staring at himself in the bathroom mirror, his gaze alighted upon a solution. With a heavy sigh, he headed back to his room for a pair of scissors, and set about shearing the thick lustrous threads that reached down to his heart. Ally's jaw dropped at the sight of his clean shaven face, opening even wider when he stretched the long strands of hair from his jacket pocket. But she was nothing if not understanding, and when he explained what they had to do, the two hurried back to the gymnasium where they sat up late into the night, weaving the whiskers into an almost exact replica of the net that had been hanging there only hours before.

When his teammates arrived the next day, all were astonished to find Bart's face bare. They wondered what had happened—was the pressure of the tournament getting to him? had he failed to connect with Ally Coop?—none suspecting what was suspended just ten feet above them.

The game got under way and Bart Jordan could not miss. He scored 20 points in the first half. What's more, his steals far exceeded even what he could do when he had been using his 'darts'. It was almost like the net, *his net*, was pulling him to it. When the teams switched sides, the eeriness stayed put. The Candles could not sink a shot to save their lives. Twice it seemed the ball had sailed through the rim only to be stopped mid-swirl and vehemently spat back out. Some even fancied they heard an accompanying belch. Every rebound found its way into Bart's hands, and he surpassed his first half scoring by five in the second, for a grand total of 45 points. The final score Agawam 75 Southwick 16.

As his teammates carried him off the court, Ally caught Bart's eye and, with an almost imperceptible nod in the direction of the net, flashed a knowing smile. It was their little secret, and with the final against the Longmeadow Larks being an away game, no one else had a reason to suspect anything for some time. The sheer momentum of The Bats explosive semi-final win over The Candles carried the team to victory again, becoming league champions in a less-lopsided match ending in Agawam 70 Longmeadow 59.

Never one to rest on his laurels, Bart resumed training the following day in Agawam gym. And feeling naked without it, he resolved to grow his beard back, though soon opting for the slimmed down tasche of years previous. As the new hair grew, so too did a strong physiopsychic connection with the strands still entwined on the metal under the backboard. Bart could not miss. So much so, that in order to make any tangible improvements during practice, he had to shoot solely on the opposite net.

When his teammates rejoined him over the summer, they began to notice this special connection with the hoop nearest their latest Champions banner. But Bart was one step ahead of them, diverting their attention by becoming a more well-rounded and sharing player overall. He would go on to lead the league in assists, a by-no-means easy feat as whenever he set foot upon the Agawam floor, he felt an almost irresistible desire to immediately grab the ball and shoot. Bart dominated every game there, never failing to rack up at least 50 points, feeding his teammates for another 20 or so. Averaging 30 points away from Agawam kept suspicions low that there might be anything exceptional about his home court advantage. But of course the hair net was starting to be noticed by the students. Its chestnut color just that much darker than the begrimed white of its counterpart across the parquet. That first night Ally had suggested dying it to match, but short on time in their novel circumstances, Bart just wanted the thing done, a good night's sleep, and perhaps other nocturnal activities more pressing before the big game. There was no way to prove anything, of course, and by now Bart's whiskers had grown back to their original length. But rumors did begin to circulate. The most popular story, whispered in hushed tones around campus, contended that it was shaved beaver fur, which sent the student body all a titter.

Bart's senior season was shaping up fine with the Bats going undefeated and Jordan himself leading the league in points, assists, and the new category of rebounds. No one on the current roster could remember a time they had lost in Agawam, nor could they recall when it wasn't a blowout. The gym resounding with so many wins, the entire Bats team—

most of whom exhibited moustaches of their own, shorter of course, as was the style then—felt a peculiar affiliation with their home turf. And the fact that one of their nets looked a bit funny only added to their affection, most even considering it a sort of good luck charm. The final against the Bondsville Specters would take place here that March. The Bats felt assured of victory.

When the day came, the team strolled onto the court only to be confronted by a most disconcerting sight. An empty space where Bart's hair had hung. Looks of panic abounded, not in the least from Bart himself, for it was obvious this was a malicious act of sabotage. From opening tip-off, things were amiss. An early breakaway saw Bart botch an easy pass, sending it clear out of bounds. Followed five minutes later by him firing an air ball from the corner over the rim and again into the crowd. He began to wonder—is the hair here? In the building somewhere, couched in the pocket of a bewitching Bondsville fan maneuvering around the bleachers, drawing his shots out like a magnet? Who would do such a thing? Bart had never known such mental anguish in his life. All he had worked for, his last college game, now about to be sent down the tubes.

At halftime, Agawam was trailing 24-20. The home crowd despaired at how such a great team could be brought so low, the mystery itself provoking further anxiety. All eyes, for reasons their owners could not explain, were drawn to the unadorned metal ring Agawam had been defending. Walking into the locker room, Bart caught sight of Allison staring up at the basket herself. Breaking her gaze, she turned to give him what she hoped was a reassuring smile. Unbeknownst to her, she bestowed upon him much more than that, as her cascade of blonde locks presented Bart with an idea. After listening to Coach Day's attempts to rally the troops, Bart discreetly grabbed a pair of cuticle scissors from the medical shelf and hurried into a bathroom stall. Snipping off the tiniest piece from each end of his new moustache, blindly trying to make the cuts symmetrical so they would go unnoticed, he cradled the hair into his palm, and returning to the court, ran to the rim to mime a lay-up, placing this tiny offering as best he could betwixt hoop and backboard. When the huddle broke, Bart stepped out onto the parquet with renewed confidence and vigor. Positively charging up and down the floor, stealing the ball left and right, and when the moment came, bringing it in close to the basket to let it roll off his fingertips at the apex of his jump. Almost as if to disturb the target as little as possible. No one questioned his delicate manner, it was working. He quickly matched his first half total of 10 points to put Agawam ahead 40-36. Jordan kept the pressure on, Bondsville unable to get the ball past him. In the closing moments of his college career Bart once again regained the white hot glory of the past two years, scoring an incredible 20 points in three minutes, bringing his game total back to the usual 50, and ending his last collegiate season, quite rightly, as a champion. Final score Agawam 88 Bondsville 40.

As fans mobbed him, Bart made his way to Allison who was also rushing down from the bleachers to reach him. Each gazed at the bare metal of the hoop, sharing its secret in the way only two lovers can. Pinching his cheek, she told him to go get changed and meet her right here afterwards. As Bart walked back into the locker room an idea struck him, pure as a swish, and he once again secreted away the cuticle scissors.

When he returned to Allison at center court, Bart dropped to one knee. "My love, will you do me the incredible honor of becoming my wife? I promise to get you a more traditional one soon, but for now . . ." and he slid a smooth sandy-colored circle over her finger, the locks above the loop knotted into a diamond shape. At the end of the summer the two were married, the reception held in the Agawam gymnasium where they had met for that first date the year before. Although Bart did eventually buy her that proper engagement ring he had promised, she preferred to wear the original one fashioned out of his hair, being appreciably more personal, unique, and possessing the vitality of a champion. With the pro basketball league having dissolved in 1904 and no other such ventures on the horizon, the couple surprised everyone by moving to Georgia to take over a Cubbins Family peach farm from a retiring uncle.

The story should end there except for that two years after Jordan's death, in 1961, a basketball net made of human hair sold at an East Bay State Sales auction for $6000 under very mystery circumstances, the company declining to provide any details regarding the seller.

Black & White & Red All Over

When Ustin Zamok was but a boy his Uncle Ilya taught him to play chess by the firelight of the family dacha. During his second ever game, Ustin picked up a pawn to advance it to c4 before deciding better of the move and returning it to its original square. His uncle went ballistic. Throwing the chess board into the fire, he ranted and raved about how this is the one thing you never do. "You place that where you originally intended to and I will take your knight!" Little Usy sat attentive in the oversized armchair, his face growing progressively more crimson through the interplay of shame and the heat of burning rooks, watching as Ilya's great beard punctuated his pronouncements until the irate man had to be physically removed from the room by his brothers. Ustin followed the men out and calmly stated his next move to his uncle, Queen to f5, carrying on from his previously supposed blunder, but now with a mate in three. You learn quickly when the board is on fire.

Despite the intensity of the evening, Ustin did not cry. Instead, he swore revenge. And in a most spectacular way. It would be some years before he faced his uncle again over the sixty-four squares but when the time came he would be ready. Since puberty, Usy, still known by his diminutive, had started cultivating his own moustache and by the age of 17 it swept down to his shoulders. The family doctor put this down to a combination of genes and the boy's love of beets. Pickled, roasted, in latkes, shred into slaw, sliced on sandwiches, and of course heavy on the borscht, both hot and cold. And when finished with these scrumptious delicacies, his lower facial features dyed that particular brand of deep red, Usy would delight in working the juices further into his skin with his fingertips, the after-meal effect looking like he'd suddenly been electrocuted whilst simultaneously applying lipstick and rouge. If glam rock had existed in the latter part of the 19th century, Usy Zamok would have been among the first strapping on a guitar. It was these, the hair-embellishing nutrients and minerals found in the beetroot extract, that the medical man credited the alarming rate at which Usy's moustache continued to expand. And for Usy, it was only after such massagings of upper lip that he would reach for a napkin, and another, and another, to wipe not face but hands clean. He did not want furry paws, for the same reason he always kept his fingernails well-trimmed—lest any part of his hand touch a chess piece unawares. But what worried physician and family was the way in which Usy would consume his beets, his food, his chess match transcripts, indeed, how he did anything. Usy had a wild competitive streak that nothing, not even beet juice, could douse. Although they did not know Usy's extended moustache was privately a direct challenge to his Uncle Ilya's beard, grown longer and from less facial space, his family did realize there was something antagonistic about it, sensed his need to have the most bountiful moustache in the area, perhaps the world. He was like this with everything. When Usy found out the great Serbian inventor Nikola Tesla used 18 napkins per meal, Usy immediately began requiring 21 such linens to accompany him at table. Though he made a show of wiping his hands and the corners of his mouth with each and every one of them, there was nothing compulsive about his cleaning. It was simply that Usy knew Tesla had a rule about his dining apparati being divisible by three, and reasoned that if he deployed anything less than the next multiple up, Tesla might decline to acknowledge it.

Nowhere was his competitive streak seen more vividly than over the chess board. Reasoning that attack was the best form of attack, in every game Usy very quickly went on the warpath. In fact he would often decorate his face with beet juice before a match, in the style of the native North American tribes he had read about in St. Petersburg's vast library, a favorite symbol being the zigzag across his forehead, representing the lightning that would grant him additional power and speed. This lasted until 1901, when all such face paint was banned from tournament play. Meanwhile, he had learned to put his lengthy moustache to another use besides simply show. Leading some to conjecture that he was overly found of the letters 'b' and 'e', though perhaps not of existence itself, using beeswax, Usy would shape the ends of his tasche into loops sturdy enough to lift and convey a chess piece across the black and white squares. It was armed with two of these that he was ready to face his uncle again. Ilya had not put in the time during the intervening years, playing, yes, but studying the game hardly at all. Usy, of course, had done little else, except eat beets. The rematch was no contest. Usy taunted his uncle every step of the way, letting his lip locks hover over, say, a bishop and then, with a flick of his head, deciding to advance a rook instead. Or encircling a pawn in this cyclone of hair, all the while holding his uncle's gaze, and repeating the words 'not touching'. Once in fact purposely grazing the horse's mane of the knight, only to have his hand swoop in simultaneously and guide its L-shaped journey kingwards. And with a final flourish, declaring checkmate after 21 moves, Usy swept the board with his whiskers to send all his uncle's pieces flying into the awaiting flames of the tableside fire.

It is not unusual for chess masters to have unusual habits, but still Usy's eccentricities loomed large, helping to make him the man to beat. And doing so became the obsession of one Igor 'Igly' Leonov. To Igly, who had lost to Zamok two years previously and knew himself to be the far inferior player, it was a matter of psychological warfare rather than any sort of skill at the game. In fact, chess itself was simply the field of a much more interior battle, which, if timed correctly, would complete its process of psychic dissolution at the exact moment Zamok noticed his king would be mated. Igly performed well enough to qualify for the 1906 tournament in Chernobyl, arriving in the city with facial hair whose length was rivaled only by Usy's own locks and, along with the rest of his scalp, dyed a deep shade of black. Not a color that would arouse suspicion, yet Leonov's motives were to align himself with the immense energy of the city and its surrounding area, 'Chernobyl' of course meaning 'black grass'.

It was Usy's habit to arrive early at such competitions, giving him the chance to go over the room with a keen eye, making sure his opponents hadn't laid any traps for him. He had never gotten over that initial surprise of his uncle suddenly sweeping a perfectly good chess board into the fire. Once satisfied with these precursory checks, Usy would make his way around the local vegetable vendors to secure supplies for his stay. He naturally traveled with just such a bounty, but besides desiring freshness, he was also curious as to what beet conglomerations might then be in vogue in each particular section of the country he visited. He would spend some time snacking upon such treats until making a final round of preliminary inspections before the start of the tournament. His usual routine was knocked off-kilter this fine Spring morning by the contents of the mail he received upon checking in to his hotel. Fan letters were by no means unusual—detailed fantasies of what mysterious members of the public would like to do to or with his luscious locks, scientific studies of what the senders termed 'criminally ignored' alternative varieties of root vegetable, a few postcards commending him on his chess play—but what stood out was the brown paper parcel with no return address and forged postmark, though this Usy did not notice, hand-delivered by a gentlemen this morning, of whom the hotel clerk was unawares, as a colleague now finished with his shift had taken reception of the, what turned out to be, book. Strolling to his room, Usy tore open the gift, his eyebrows jumping to high heaven. The accompanying letter proclaimed this to be a recently discovered work of the great Russian master, published privately in accordance with his wishes upon his death—Gogol's *We Got The Beet*. The letter was signed with an illegible scribble but Usy's interest was piqued. He made his way to scrutinize the tournament tables with the hefty volume under his arm.

Igor Leonov turned his face back around the corner from which he had been watching, smiling to himself. The mind games had begun. He continued to shadow Usy at a distance, delighting in Zamok's perusal of the ersatz edition. Indeed Usy seemed positively absorbed by the book as, with his safety checks completed, he sat devouring both it and a copious amount of beet tartare. Igly knew the man to be hypervigilant, and even with being so engrossed in the tome as he was, Usy would not fail to notice, and begin to be unnerved by, the puzzled stares of passersby. With any luck, a stranger might question the validity of Usy's reading material, causing the latter to become distressed by his own explanations. But there were other matters to deal with even if this did not to come to pass.

As spectators and players alike shuffled into the hall, Usy had for quite a while been sympathizing with Petrovich's quest to secure textile dyes from the Prizrak beet farm whilst simultaneously planning to take over that concern and expand his business to include the manufacturing of his own brand of molasses. Sticky stuff. Usy barely glanced up from the pages as tournament favorite, the Italian Antonioni, strolled in followed by Geneva's Hadron, another master likely to go far this competition. But with the room almost full, Usy's intuitive senses pricked up when the doors opened upon a confident Igly pausing to take in the scene.

"Imposter!" Usy jumped from his seat aghast, gesticulating wildly to the arbiter. "Bar that man!" Igly Leonov indulged a small smile as he proceeded to enter the arena amidst such an eruption. He was off to a strong start.

Usy busied himself passionately explaining to the referee that he had seen this very contestant lose ignobly seven months ago in Chelyabinsk and that Igly had had the cleanest face he had ever laid eyes on. Skin of alabaster so shiny, it was barely conceivable that hair could poke its way through. There was no way this charlatan could have grown a moustache to such a scale in only 200 odd days. The hair, he insisted, must be fake. It took some time for the governing committee to make Usy understand that there were currently no rules against participating with a false beard.

Sitting down over the board, Igly, with the luck of the regional color, had drawn black. And so had every opportunity to mirror his opponent's moves. Of course any good chess player can dismantle this strategy quickly, but Usy was not himself, unnerved by everything that had occurred with Leonov already. The sight of this man, yes, but on a much subtler level, and one he couldn't possibly know was the work of this adversary, by what Usy had been reading in *We Got The Beet*. The exploits of the two scientists, Fyodor and Nikolai, each the double of the other, working so assiduously on Prizrak's farm. Nikolai tending to the roots from a subterranean lab while Fyodor followed him everywhere, taking copious notes of such experiments, hoping to publish should these undertakings to revolutionize the beet field, in every sense of the word, prove successful. But whose name would go on the final paper? It was not at all clear, especially as the two men's personas began to merge, ever more enmeshed together. There was a strong possibility that Prizrak, as financier, might step in and claim credit, or even Petrovich, who was working furtively with the famed Dr. Dreysky. Usy kept catching himself wondering how it would all play out, and if this could facilitate a real world transformation of beets as we know them. Already he was beginning to crack, periodically placing his hands in front of his face, like a child when it does not want to be seen. Igly began doing the same.

Full of his own self-worth, Usy did not bother with learning the names of his competitors. He knew their souls, as expressed through tormented eyes during the throes of a game. What hidden, unspeakable, darknesses lay there that, by their very nature, could not so easily be put into words. When interlocutors failed to understand the strange utterances he gave when trying to capture this essence in order to refer to this or that player, Usy resorted to attempting to translate these into a sort of pantomime, which did not make things any clearer. This is all by way of saying that Ustin Zamok may not have been aware that most called Igor Leonov by the diminutive 'Igly', which of course means 'needles'. Igly himself, who had studied the man thoroughly before this meeting in Chernobyl, was mindful there was a strong chance the master would not even know his name, but sat twisting the ends of his great moustache into the finest tips he could anyways, as if to focus some dark magic across the squares. Usy held his hands out further away from his face, as if channeling the vision of future celebrities shouting 'no photos please!' as they pushed their way through suffocating crowds full of cameras and press. Play adjourned at 10 p.m., Usy at the point of collapse.

Igly strode in the next day chomping down on a raw beet. It was almost too tough to chew but worth the effort as he watched blood vessels in Usy's face rush to the skin to match the vegetable's color. Although Usy was sure he did not have any whole raw beets in his vast store of snacks, he insisted on calling a delay to the game until he could return to his hotel and verify that Igly, 'or one of his minions', had not ransacked his supply while he was away. The much put-upon arbiter agreed, he had dealt with Zamok on many an occasion. As Usy had memorized the contents of his luggage, this did not take long, and he soon returned to the hall, albeit still steaming. Igly sat calmly in front of the board, chomping reverberating bite after reverberating bite of his beet. As the heavy crunch of such mastications echoed through the otherwise silent chamber, Usy grew weary, shouting from the doorway, "Don't you see?! He's trying to absorb my prowess."

Usy won the first game, though not by as wide of a margin as the betting man amongst the audience had wagered. Igly recognized it was going to be a difficult path to victory, but he was determined to hang in there. As the second match commenced, Igly's coach began passing him what Usy immediately identified as beet chips, stopping play to have these inspected. Finding no obvious messages written on them, Usy ran his fingers along the one Igly had just received, checking for braille or similarly encoded language that could be read by the tongue. Igly waited patiently, knowing how to force his hand. After he consumed the comestible, making a show of indulgent swallows, he settled in to move his pieces at speed, capriciously even, as if the chips had been drugged. Sensing this, Usy again halted proceedings and asked for the confiscation of said chips and in fact all Leonov's foodstuffs to be sent to a laboratory and checked for stimulants or any of the various mind-altering substances of China and South America that sometimes bestow on the nibbler tremendous visions. In a moment of great vulnerability, he leaned across the table and asked Igly, "How can you sully the beet so, sir?" This match, and the next, ended in stalemate. And as play was accelerated now, while feigning being under the influence as Usy grew ever more erratic in his responses, Igly managed a quick victory in the fourth game.

With things all tied up, the next win would decide who advances in the tournament. As the event sprung into life on this third day, for the first time in his career, Usy had not been the first to arrive at the hall. Instead of studying or getting a restorative night's sleep, he had stayed up into the small hours finishing the 888 pages of what purported itself to be Gogol's lost masterpiece. Only once he had closed its thick cover with a whimsical sigh did he allow himself to sink into dreams, visions of sugar beets dancing in his head, inaugurating a bright future for all. These fantasies buoyed him through the morning as he dressed and sat down to a beet omelet and beets on toast.

When he did enter the venue, still with plenty of time but already teeming at three-quarters full capacity, abuzz with speculation over the outcome of the board, what lay before Usy froze him to his very soul. Sitting so as to directly face him, again at his position behind the black pieces, was Igly, looking well-rested and freshly shaven. Usy made a great mental effort not to give in, but what he saw next was to be his undoing.

With five minutes until play would begin, five gentlemen dressed all in black slipped through the doors, taking seats so as to appear to Usy over Igly's right shoulder. Immediately Usy's eyes shot open what felt like miles high as his nostrils flared to the ends of the earth. The party was arranged in such an order so that the occupant of the innermost chair bore a black moustache extensive enough to rival Usy's own. The man to his right sat thoughtlessly stroking one of similar shade but of a length almost exactly half of his compatriot's walruslike whiskers. And so on. Usy's pupils slowing rolling across this field growing more monstrous by the millimeter, until it came to rest at the gentleman on the far right who possessed what anyone else would consider a perfectly normal moustache. So great was his rage, Usy could not stop shaking. He poured himself a large glass of beet juice and commenced gargling with it, for what purpose no one could be sure. Forcing himself at length to swallow, he could not escape the fact that he appeared to be seeing red. A trick of the juice in the light, perhaps? The hue began to merge with the chess board in front of him as if it were on fire, like one he had witnessed so many years before. With great effort he steadied himself and played his first move—e4. With a studied nonchalance, Igly rapidly responded with e5. Usy let out deep bellows of breath and, after some time spent with head down blocking out everything but the two royal households before him, advanced his knight to c3. Again, barely had he let go of this piece than Igly jumped his own knight to f6. Usy feeling some semblance of control now flicked his bishop up to c4. Glancing over his left shoulder, Igly then captured Usy's e4 pawn with his knight. Instead of noting what had just occurred on the board, Usy followed Igly's initial gaze, and when his eyes hit upon the black clad gentleman at the end of the facial hair processional, this figure returned his stare with an almost imperceptible smile as he raised his right hand and peeled off his moustache.

The effect on Usy was devastating. Away to the door he flew like a flash. And although those in the hall waited hours, the organizers even eventually sending out a search party, Usy never did return to the grounds or the great game of chess. Igly was declared the winner by default, though it would be Antonioni who would go on to sweep this particular tournament.

The tale of disturbed former chess champion Ustin Zamok is not as tragic as it would first appear. Using *We Got The Beet* as a springboard, he began his own experiments, keeping meticulous diary entries in the face of all who were calling him insane, and went on to innovate much in the growth and preparation of his favorite vegetable, founding financially successful lines of distribution, even making his way westward to start again in Germany and then France after the Soviets seized control of his farms in 1918. Igly Leonov may have facilitated a victory at Chernobyl 1906, but those who are familiar with the whole of the legend know his success wasn't as clear-cut black and white.

Putting The 'Ache' In Moustache

It is fitting that a dispute over the property line of a barber shop should result in a hair-razing solution. To Shave & To Hold—the V of its logo naturally upturned into an open pair of scissors—is a popular gentlemen's haircutting establishment serving the denizens of Arnhem, New York and environs. Edward van der Haar, its likeable proprietor, watches over the small but welcoming waiting area, always full of a steady stream of fellows to-be-fashioned. However, in the year 1972, TisTasche as it was then becoming known, following on from '2S2H', found itself in legal difficulties after a state zoning survey found the little shop to be straddling the new border between the townships of Arnhem and neighboring Zeeland. Van der Haar, a long-time resident of Arnhem, felt no particular allegiance to the place, cautious against any such sentiment repelling his clients from other climes. Besides being an artist of both the conventional cut and the coiffure, he considered himself a keen businessman and knew that in crisis there is also opportunity. An idea rarely put into use in the world of gentlemen's haircutting, the accidents of punk rock still some years away, but the few instances he had dealt with an enbubblegummed head or the deflated arrogance of the would-be self-stylist had convinced him of the adage's truth. Still, just how to exploit his current predicament escaped him. That is until the day Mason Stringfellow and Dick Sunderland—two athletic young lads, loyal customers since their first ever trims and now home from their freshman years at college—sat flipping through slightly-out-of-date magazines awaiting their turns in the chair and reminiscing about the various feats of strength they had witnessed on campus. Faced with the prospect of a summer break bleak from the absence of university sports, these stories were punctuated by anxious sighs to get back to the games. They chatted away, unconcerned about the hours passing or the customers ahead, for they had arrived early expressly for the purpose of catching up with each other and whomever else happened to be there, telling tale of push-ups with full kegs on their backs, hockey games that went into sextuple overtime and the hangovers that ensued, and, as van der Haar began wiping off the seat in preparation for Stringfellow's cut, a most grueling tug of war contest. Van der Haar, of course, played it cool.

The next day the barber phoned the state official in charge of this awkward dilemma of architectural division, with almost exactly half of To Shave & To Hold falling into each zone, and asked for a meeting with him and the council members of both Arnhem and Zeeland. He was nothing if not thorough, running the gamut from A to Z, as it were. After pleading his case that the building housing his business had become a beloved landmark over two decades of steady patronage, that his feelings for the place prevented him from even considering moving elsewhere, and heaven forbid any talk of tearing it down enter his thoughts, he set about making it very clear that what he had in mind could bring in a pleasant injection of cash for all involved. When he got to this last point, the town officials, being town officials, pricked up their ears.

And so the advertisements began, months in advance of the big day, the two tourist boards reaching far and wide with their promotions. Barbershop quartet spots were regularly run on the radio, and quite effectively. For even if you possess shelves overflowing with the recorded output of such musical groups, the four-part harmony evocation of a moustache-entangled tug of war is enough to give anyone pause as its message sinks in. Yes, To Shave & To Hold's cartographic fate would be decided by tug of war. And not just any tug of war. Eight men from each municipality would wind their moustaches—all of which van der Haar had lovingly tended to over the years—into the competition rope. The winning team would then lay claim to van der Haar's business. The losers would be shaven clean. Van Dyke Park, its fields within view of the shop, would play host to the match, the cord's center mark placed over the current town border, giving participants a real sense of pulling the premises into their own territory.

After years spent prepping men of all ages to look their best for whatever activities they may be pursuing, van der Haar instinctively knew how to put on a good show. The grounds were lined with food and merchandise vendors, and the staffs of the packed local hotels, for a modest consideration of course, had done a great job of ushering attendees out several hours early in order to be cajoled into spending the maximum amount of money at the park. The stalls were covered with sets of fake moustache and cord combinations, while above them hung t-shirts, mugs, hats, tea towels, you name it, with an artist's depiction of To Shave & To Hold being stretched to bursting by beroped moustaches, complete with date and the names of all involved. There was also a secret stash van der Haar had furtively ordered—half declaring Arnhem, half stating Zeeland as its rightful residence—to be put out for sale immediately following the final whistle.

With the skirmish due to start at 1 p.m., under a clear beautiful sky, pre-show entertainment was provided by children from the nearby school districts Double Dutching with a facsimile of the official game equipment, wearing vests with wide vertical stripes, boater hats, and custom fake moustaches of red, white, and blue, the colors of both America and Holland. Spectators had long-since seated themselves on all the available orange crates set up across the grass, placed to give a village feel as well as saving money on the cost of bleachers. The public relations people had done their job well, this peculiar event drawing a sizable crowd, estimated to be at least one thousand, with interested parties—themselves exhibiting the most impressive designer stubble—having driven in from Brooklyn and Rochester, taken trains from Atlanta as well as the Portlands of both Maine and Oregon, and with planes also arriving at New York City terminals containing attendees from Seattle, Tucson, and in one case, via a long trans-Atlantic flight, the Amsterdam of the old country. The teams themselves stood warming up under the shade of some beech trees towards the outskirts of the field, bedecked in their simple but elegant uniforms—jersey and matching socks in red for Zeeland, blue for Arnhem, each featuring a variation on the Dutch lion, holding taut ropes instead of the traditional sword and arrows. The two creatures looked remarkably alike bar the gradient and twirl of the beasts' new moustaches. Arnhem's aggressive upside-down V formed an A with the animal's outstretched tongue, while Zeeland's stache flourished out, flowing longer down the body into a windblown Z. The players themselves, though soon to be disheveled, had waxed their whiskers into stunning points, now sparkling underneath the midday Sun.

Although there were at least twenty men per town whose facial hair reached far enough to render them eligible, the official rules state that tug of war is to be waged eight versus eight. After initial try-outs, van der Haar personally vetting who would coach, such a competition being uncharted territory with only the barber himself comprehending what he had in mind, sixteen of the most hefty hirsute were chosen for each side. The official eight plus a full roster of alternates in case any injuries arose ahead of time. With tug of war there is always the danger of severed arms and fingers requiring amputation, and with van der Haar's new twist on the age-old game, there would also be the additional risk of sprained facial muscles and possibly gnarlier, unforeseen, accidents.

At 12:45, in his capacity as impartial referee, van der Haar began walking the line, studiously checking to make sure each tasche was firmly tied to the rope before the contest commenced. The men narrowed their focus to join face with fight. Other than the fact that their skulls were secured to the cord, the match would follow official tug of war rules. It would be an underarm pull, though they needn't worry about a call of 'foul' for anyone's elbows dropping below their knees. With upper lips attached like so, the cable was naturally held closer to chin than chest, heads bent to prevent, as much as possible, the ensuing facial pain.

After a rather moving speech detailing his boundless love of his business and the importance of what the crowd was about to witness, van der Haar blew the whistle and the teams dug in. Despite having practiced for weeks against their reserves, today took the intensity up a great many notches. With such high stakes there in front of them, the men grappled with all their might. Legs and biceps bulged but nowhere was the strain more apparent than around the mouth and eyes. As training sessions had been closed to the public, the audience was seeing such a sight for the first time, and most were not prepared for the distress it brought them. Several men and women fainted, having to be carried to the medical tents it was believed the actual participants would rather need. But as the struggle wore on, the fascination of ever-stretching cheeks and tear-streamed eyes, shades of red and amounts of sweat hithertofore unseen, complete with otherworldly grunts, drew the crowd in further. Audible gasps and wild winces at each consecutive lean and pivot, van der Haar taking it all in like some deranged circus master. Finally, after three minutes and thirty-three seconds, like the needle scratching off the final rotation of a seven-inch pop single, Arnhem were sent catapulting, crashing and colliding over the Zeeland line. Wild cheers erupted as many of the competitors, on both sides, vomited into the mud. The mayor of Zeeland rushing out onto the field to congratulate his men who were now faced with the task of untethering themselves from the rope that had brought them so much pain and glory. Truth be told, they momentarily envied their Arnhem opponents who were simply having their staches snipped off, to then roll away, heads clutched in hands, trying to stem the uncontrollable tears of shame and more immediate physical agony.

Such sensations would not be left alone to vanish so privately, however. The advertising campaign had explicitly stated that the losing team were to have their locks sheared. And so players soon hobbled to the podium, helped by friend and foe alike, for none were immune to the creases of strain etched upon these warriors' features. The tested strands, clipped so decisively to free them, had been discreetly collected by one Harold Broome, an associate of van der Haar hired expressly for this purpose, as the business/showman had yet further plans for this most singular of community fêtes. Van der Haar himself presently reappeared, bedecked in snazzy new apron carrying a silver tray upon which sat large foaming bowl, brush, and blade, to begin ceremoniously shaving the eight members of the defeated Arnhem squad. Few knew as well as he did what this act meant to those upon whom it was being perpetrated, having nurtured these moustaches since their very first sproutings, but van der Haar valiantly held these sentiments at bay, performing the ritual with enough flair to keep the crowd engaged, eating, drinking, and buying the merchandise, bringing money into his pockets. With just the right touch of theatricality however, as the now bare-faced Arnhem lineup stepped down from the podium, van der Haar permitted himself a tiny tear, wiped arcingly from his cheek with a sweep of the apron.

Next up, the Zeeland champions took their places to heady applause, heavily talcum-powdered skin obscured by prominent V-for-Victory moustaches, freshly waxed upright. After a moment, van der Haar joined them front and center to be presented with the legal documents that henceforth made him one of their own. And just when it seemed they had reached an emotional climax, van der Haar feigned surprise as Harold Broome wound his way to the podium to gift him the competition rope. The barber again affecting astonishment as he held the cord aloft for all to see, asking Broome knowingly if the darker-colored strands towards it center were indeed what he thought they were. Broome confirming that yes, there lay the collective former facial hair of the entire Arnhem team. The Arnhem crew themselves—busy applying copious amounts of aloe to their overstressed skin in the hopes of assuaging what further damage shaving had brought—paused to reflect that at least their tasches would live on, one even heard to mysteriously mutter "it's not goodbye, it's 'til we meet again'." As a parting gesture before the festivities came to a close, van der Haar announced that he would hang this prize above the mirrors of To Shave & To Hold, a cherished souvenir of a most memorable day.

The event was such a success, it is probable that, even without the residents of Arnhem grumbling about revenge, van der Haar would start to think about staging it again. A rematch. One to be played in perpetuity, forever delayed of a permanent decision. And why not? Both towns, as well as the restaurants, bars, and hotels of nearby De Groot, and even out as far as Spelbos, had profited from the proceedings. Chuckling to himself en route to the bank the following Monday morning, van der Haar could only see two obstacles to organizing another contest the following year. The first being that Arnhem had forfeited the vital equipment they would need to participate. These men's moustaches had been entwined with their lives for much longer than they had been with any rope. It had taken a great deal of time to grow them to such expanses and getting back to regulation length within the short span of a year was highly doubtful. The second hindrance was that To Shave & To Hold now legally belonged to Zeeland. The whole point of the match had been to decide where in the state zoning structure it fell.

Having made his deposit, van der Haar was still pondering the possibilities on his way to To Shave & To Hold, when he ran into Skip Tweede, and was shocked to see the extent of this man's Handlebar. Why hadn't Tweede taken part on Saturday? And if he had, why hadn't he been sheared? Van der Haar began to panic. He had been so meticulous with every detail, could he really have missed this? It was only after a moment of cold sweats that van der Haar remembered. In the interest of keeping the focus on the eight who had competed, as well as not wanting to milk the ceremony too long and thus run the risk of losing the crowd's attention, Arnhem's second unit had not been invited onto the podium. There had been no reason for them to even suit up as there could be no substitutions once the war had gotten underway. A coin-shaped lightbulb went off over van der Haar's head. There was still a full set of players, already trained, who were ready to go. They could stage the rematch tomorrow if they liked. Plus there were alternates walking around Arnhem who, for whatever reasons, hadn't been seen on either side of the rope first time around. Van der Haar was positively beaming when he eventually entered his shop.

The second hurdle seemed less of a mountain to climb now. After all, he had the ropes. Striking while the iron was hot, with all involved still agog at just how much money they'd made on a single Saturday, van der Haar called a meeting with the district councils again. While some Zeeland residents were naturally dubious about the possibility of relinquishing the title and the glory, others argued passionately that there was no reason why they couldn't win it again, raking in more of both, and of course a barrage of banknotes to boot. With the help of lawyers representing the many parties, and having to bring the state zoning official in for a cut, an irregular tax scheme was introduced whereby To Shave & To Hold would be legally located in the winning township for the duration of one year following the decision of each match. Van der Haar's earnings in his capacity as barber were nothing to scoff at but what he would take in from just the one day of the contest proved any additional paperwork to be a mere trifle of an annoyance. The same went for all the community officials as, if last Saturday's activities could be counted upon to continue, tourists would flock to the hotels, restaurants, bars, and boutiques of Arnhem, Zeeland, and the surrounding municipalities spending money hand over fist.

And so in 1973, on the third Saturday in July, the date on which the boundary dispute would annually occur moving forward, the teams gathered again, jerseys tweaked to even more valiant lions, and with many more varied vendors selling their wares in and around the vicinity of Van Dyke Park. Record shop stalls specializing in candy-striped songsmiths laid out their vinyl, members of Here & Now Meditation Center passed out pamphlets, even a purveyor of toy tugboats and stuffed rabbits flogged his wares. The orange crates were replaced by more conventional sports seating, and this investment in bleachers proved worthwhile as the crowd more than doubled this year for the first ever rematch. Skip Tweede found himself captaining the Arnhem squad of mostly, if not fresh, then new faces, although the previous year's participants Theodore Scheren and Dweezil Knevel (no relation), through a diet almost exclusively consisting of spinach, tangerines, almonds, and walnuts, had grown their hair back long enough to qualify for the second unit.

In Zeeland, too, new players were anxious to make their name in the sport. Courtesy dictated that the original eight would carry on, and of course they had the advantage of growing their hair that much longer, but after a series of secret meetings, the athletics department also began to hold try-outs for a relief lineup of their own, covert affairs conducted in rooms unknown-to-most below the gymnasium, far from spying Arnhem eyes. Anything could happen in a year, and they wanted to keep To Shave & To Hold well within their borders.

The atmosphere twelve months on was as tense as the cord stretched taut over the center line. Each town having everything to strive for. Van der Haar, now in a gold top hat with matching cape and scepter, paced the formation again checking the fibers and facial connections, often giving these a tap with his stick, before promptly blowing his, again gold, whistle at 1 p.m. Bracing themselves, the rivals dug in, trading slip and recovery after slip and recovery until they were well past the 3 minutes 33 seconds of last year's final time. The strain on their faces was unbelievable, causing many in the crowd to again faint and be carried away, even those accustomed to the sight from the previous skirmish. But there was much more at stake now, and he who has a why to live can bear almost any how. As the six minute mark approached, Bob 'Slappy' Rust collapsed in the middle of Zeeland's squad, followed seconds later by Chris Kussen on the Arnhem half. The two slumped over the rope, attached by their faces, red and raw, thankfully still breathing, but adding appreciable extra weight to each side. Skip Tweede, anchoring for Arnhem, realized that if such a thing were to happen to him—and the likelihood felt uncomfortably close—his men would topple over the mark. He drew an almighty breath and, heaving with everything he had, shouted 'Pull!' It was enough. With a determination none were sure from whence it came, as the stopwatch read 6:19, Arnhem hoisted Zeeland over the line. Before the whistle finished sounding, both teams collapsed in tears. Zeeland were cut free, with the medics racing to revive Chris Kussen. They knew in their hearts he would be furious if so much as one hair was plucked from his victorious tasche.

And so To Shave & To Hold returned to Arnhem. Van der Haar commenting to himself, 'home again, but surely not for long.' In fact, the shop seems to swing like a pendulum, from A–Z, beginning to end and back again, fate decreeing it never stays in one town for more than a period of three years. And bringing ever more tourism and attention to the area. Children who have grown up in De Groot and Spelbos, even in some cases from the larger cities beyond, have migrated to Arnhem and Zeeland in the hopes of trying their hands and faces in the tournament. The game rope, its girth having grown considerably from all the accumulated hair over the years, is these days kept on display in the winning side's courthouse, folded several times over upon itself before being styled into an Imperial moustache and placed above the lip of the giant portrait of van der Haar that hangs in both entryways. Van der Haar has continued to bolster the event, with Van Dyke Park undergoing expansions over the years, pre- and post- show activities now including circus acts, famous rock and jazz band combos, as well as artistic renderings, both live action and more permanent reproductions, of contests past. Ever the self-promoter, van der Haar undertakes interviews and photo shoots whenever he can, and when recently asked by the New Groningen Gazette if he felt any differences between being stationed in Arnhem or Zeeland, replied 'a few, but I don't like to split hairs.'

The Wizard of Wycombe

From the time he first learned to speak, William Wegmuller loved the fact that he came from Wycombe. All those W's! Which is also the first letter of the word 'wings', his favorite object to draw. He would sit at the family table for hours covering page upon page with primitive symbols of birds flying off at every angle. The funny thing was that he would start by drawing a regular picture—a house, some figures in its yard, the Sun beaming down upon them, etc. Then he would grab his black paint and douse the scene with a fluster of feathers that seemed to come right at you, closing down your peripheral vision. And these were always in the shape of his initials. Only he could tell where he signed a piece, which, with his love of his name, how could he not? Others opted to depict such airborne creatures, if they painted them at all, as variations of a V. This observation occasionally gave young William pause for thought. After all, his grandfather still pronounced Wegmuller in the European style, rather than as its more rounded English cousin. But to William, one could do so much more with a W, greater than the twice implied, stretching out each side to one's wont.

Shortly after his 10th birthday, the sport of badminton was sweeping the area and, hearing tale of its birdie, William was intrigued. Giving the game a go, he found he immensely enjoyed being out on the grass with his racket. Until he noticed something. No matter how he hit it—with a striking sweep or a soft flick of the wrist—the shuttlecock's trajectory invariably described the shape of a U. There was no abrupt change of course mid-air that would even approach a V, let alone the W shapes he had been committing to paper for as long as he could remember. He walked off the makeshift court, sat under the nearest dogwood tree, and began to ponder this conundrum. When the picnic was over his grandfather came to retrieve him, William attempting to explain what now raged inside his young mind. His grandfather listened, keeping silent about his own dropping of the familial umlaut upon arrival in America. That would only complicate the issue.

Though he reached no definite conclusion about the essence of art, its representation of the natural world, and how it all relates to him and his name, William continued to contemplate, examine, even brood over the situation. Which involved a lot of unconscious stroking of his chin. And it is this act that most residents of Wycombe credit with the boy's early development and abnormally fast growth of his legendary beard. By the age of 19 such strands hung copiously over his heart, its shape amorphous, an echo of William's inner turmoil, not a soul in the outside world able to decide whether it delineated a U or a V, no matter how many times he ran a comb or brush through it.

By now his artwork had taken a drastic turn towards the unconventional. He would spend hours carefully crafting the most intricate of worlds—lurid steps of gold abruptly ending in infinite jagged corners, spectral walls that barely contained amorphous chaos, butterflies and their pursuers enmeshed within the same net—only to then grab the black paint and splatter an avian legion over these most impressionistic scenes of his inner life. He whimsically signed his W.W. in a deep navy blue woven seamlessly into the scene. Gallery viewers likened it to glimpsing a director who is rumored to appear in his own films.

But William was not one of those artists who spend all day indoors, never letting the sunshine soak into their skin. No, he had also become equally as obsessed with badminton. In clement weather he could be found on the lawn with a racket in his hand, obsessing over the arc of his volley. Of course the hairpin net shot comes the closest to approximating a V, and it was for this reason that William favored playing as near to the center as possible. He was once heard stating that he would know the woman he was to marry by her returning this shot to him in kind, thereby tracing a double-u, emphasis on the 'u', and even better if it was then repeated, sketching out his initials, and also those of Wonder Woman, who such a lass, oh boy, she must surely be.

There was also the notion of interference, for thwacking the shuttle off an intervening body gave William the V he was looking for. A smash that resulted in the birdie spiking back up off the ground at a similar angle being more pleasing to

William for the shape it implied than the point it scored. He wrote letter after letter to various badminton committees extolling the virtues of purposefully hitting a volley into the post to have it arc off onto the opponent's side of the court. These were often accompanied by petitions for a change to the rulebook awarding this shot an extra point. His reasoning being that such a maneuver should be applauded for its daring, as there was a much greater risk of sending it out of bounds.

And dangerous it was, for as William was out practicing solo one day, preparing for his first ever tournament, while attempting to put more spin on his overhead shot off the post, he miscalculated how far back to bring his swing, walloping himself behind the ear with the side of his racket in the process. Down he went like a lead pelican. When he came to, some moments later, he did so with caution, noticing that right in the middle of his bountiful beard, sat a peaceful cedar waxwing staring at him, head cocked to one side. It did not move as, with the greatest of care, William—slowly, silently—sat up. Although it could have easily been raiding the collection of hair for material to build a nest, the bird gave no indication of doing so, seeming to have already found a fully formed home.

Rubbing the emerging egg on his skull, William got up and went back to work. The waxwing stayed with him. Balanced easily within the abundant hair covering William's chest, the little thing showed no signs of leaving. Later that evening, as William set brush to paper, an occasional approving chirp emanated from below William's chin and traveled up to his ears. The sandwich he absentmindedly ate while he painted, as well as the accumulation from all its predecessors, provided more than enough crumbs for the creature's sustenance, and

William noted the waxwing still nestled close to his heart when he took to bed.

The day of the tournament arrived. 'Bandit', as William had affectionately designated his new winged friend after the rich black strip around its eyes, was still with him. Now William, due to his irregular appearance, soapbox stance on his favorite shot, and quirky artistic nature, was already known as something of a maverick in the small but budding world of Pennsylvania badminton. But even he knew that such a presence on the pitch might be frowned upon. He was not a pirate. Neither, despite its name, was Bandit. Nor, for that matter, was Bandit a parrot. Not that there were special exemptions for these. But Bandit instinctively sensed this predicament, and although William could still feel the bird within his beard, when he looked in the mirror to check his sweatbands, the waxwing was nowhere to be seen.

Bandit remained hidden throughout the match, which William easily won 21-13. Returning to the park's public rest area, today doubling as a makeshift locker room, however, William soon noticed not one but two heads poking out of his beard. Unbeknownst to him, a wren had somehow joined Bandit within William's plentiful hair sometime during play. There was little William could do about it now. Let the officials sort it out if they objected, William had a second match to prepare for. Though sure enough, when he headed back out onto the court, both birds dutifully tucked themselves out of view.

Smokey, as the wren was christened due to the abundance of grey encircling its small face, easily settled into the lower reaches of William's beard, making due with the tiniest food particles that, having fallen the furthest, could be found inside. There was certainly enough room without either feeling crowded. The two had remained hidden throughout the second preliminary round, emerging once again now that William was back home and sitting at his table in front of his brushes and tubes of color. He looked about him at all the thick black strokes of wings that covered the portraits that covered the walls. Could these—like the earliest cave drawings depicting, what else, but the animals the artist desired to hunt—have been a primitive yet unintentional form of magic? Summoning what William put down on the page? There were certainly enough of them, a focused and sustained effort spanning many years. William was more than a little shaken. Smokey and Bandit stayed quiet.

After the initial horror of the possibilities of his own power had passed, William considered its potency. If he had, though he was by no means sure of this, somehow brought the situation into being, perhaps he could harness such means for his own advantage. He set about sketching the scene of his victory tomorrow, the final shot banking off the right post, traveling in a perfect V to land untouched at his rival's feet for point 21. So caught up was he, and with the birds keeping stumm in his beard, it was only after a quarter of the canvas had been slathered in thick black W's that he snapped himself out of his robotic adherence to process.

Taking the court the following day for the semi-final, William swallowed copiously at the sight across the lawn. His challenger was exactly as he had depicted him the night before—thick eyeglasses, yellow shirt, shorts with an argyle spanning the spectrum of blue, and holding the racket in his left hand. As the match got underway, this man proved a tougher adversary than his previous two. William's faith in the sure win foretold by his painting soon shaken by the rockets his opponent was firing at the net, close enough to shave any unruly threads right off. He felt Smokey and Bandit begin to stir. And then with the score tied 17-all, a great rush of wings raced into the surrounding sky, swooping down to accompany William's next serve. Mr. Argyle had no chance to even see the birdie concealed amidst the moving mass of feathers. The judges, claiming an 'act of God', tossed William another shuttle to repeat the serve. But when the same thing happened five times in a row over the course of 20 minutes, they threw up their hands, completely flummoxed. In all the excitement, Smokey and Bandit presently took to the edges of William's beard, joined by three more fowl of a smaller variety. These latest arrivals being differentiated by their shades of olive green, warm reddish-brown, and frosty white, and the newly formed quintet were doing plenty of chirping. When William made to serve again, the line judge pointed out the five fowl sitting in his beard, at which William only shrugged. The sky remained clear as the single birdie traveled across, an anxious Argyle by now too frazzled to return its service. And thus the game swooped to its conclusion, Argyle never quite recovering enough to snatch another point from the talons of defeat.

Back home once again with brush in hand, William bestowed nicknames upon his new companions, who also seemed intent on staying. The olive warbler became Frog, which amused them both, the white-breasted nuthatch was obviously Snowman, and as he first confused the eastern towhee with another of the redbreasted variety, William dubbed this one Robinson. Twirling the brush in and out of his beard absentmindedly but much to his little tenants' delight, William appraised his painting of the previous evening. Had the fact that it was semi-splattered in wings been the cause of what happened in the match that day? Had he summoned this peculiar force of nature? Nothing like this had ever appeared before, so was an accumulation of all his years of painting now bursting through at once? Taking no chances, he again commenced sketching his victory for the morrow, catching himself just in time as he automatically began to paint a giant wing above the center line. Smokey, Robinson, Bandit, Frog, and Snowman chorused their excitement, and with such encouragement, William fleshed out that partial W shape into 'William Wegmuller Wins!'

With all five birds nestled unseen in his beard, William walked out on the court for the final. Word had spread overnight of the previous day's proceedings, and the stands which had been half full at best were now overflowing with expectant citizens awaiting another spectacle from the oddball Wegmuller. William sensed this too, especially as there was the distinct feel of disappointment in the air as he raised his racket to serve at his 20-16 game point. The bleachers had already started to empty and even his especially forceful spike off the post, while winning him the tournament, failed to bring any enthusiasm from the crowd. Snowman and Bandit poked their heads out and a woman approaching the exit stopped in her tracks, shouting 'There they are!' Going with the flow, Frog, Smokey, and Robinson, emerged as well, chirping their little heads off. Soon the rush that fans had been pining for swooped about the sky. A dazzling cloud of wings descending to lift the medal off the champion's shoulders before arranging themselves above the net in the triple W outline of 'William Wegmuller Wins!'. The spectators stood awestruck for a moment as the enormity of the event told hold, then letting loose wild laughter, shrieks, and cheers, spontaneous outbreaks of dancing, and much flashing of camera bulbs as the flock joined in with the crowd, to fly amidst joyous faces, perch upon shoulders, perform tricks for the photographers, all the while singing their own sweet song of merriment.

There was a fair amount of conjecture in the regional newspapers the following week, though reporters quickly tired of attempting to interview William, who wisely refused them entry into his home, closing the blinds against all peeping would-be art critics, and consistently feigned ignorance as to why Mother Nature should be showing such an interest in his badminton career. Its own trajectory beginning to bloom, with offers for future competitions pouring in daily. Initially, promoters seemed unable to understand that William could not guarantee the appearance of the birds, but even despite having to be written out of the contracts, the avian population of eastern Pennsylvania still dutifully arrived at every match. Though exactly when and how they would show always remained a mystery, and thus a delight.

While William stalled investigations into the phenomenon for as long as he could, it was only a matter of time before a snoop from the *Bucks County Heresay* found some childhood paintings done by Wegmuller that had once hung in the neighboring Wrightstown library, filed and almost forgotten in a dusty old cabinet in its basement. Though they were only three birdscapes in cardboard frames, the paper used these as a springboard to run a piece about the presence of the supernatural in the area, pointing out that the front left side of the Wycombe rail station looks suspiciously like a wizard's hat.

Outed, William decided to own it. He opened his doors to one and all who wished to see his creations. The few scenes not covered in black wings were easily spun as him sketching his victories after the fact. He wasn't going to completely give the game away. He had a headpiece especially designed for him modeled on that very section of Wycombe's stationhouse roof. Although too cumbersome to wear whilst knocking shuttlecocks to and fro, he nevertheless took to walking around town showing it off, Smokey, Bandit, Snowman, Frog, Robinson and two new additions—Port, a thusly colored young grosbeak, and Starbird, a goldfinch with a five pointed dark patch over its right eye—all visible within his beard. Gallery owners from Philadelphia, Baltimore, and Brooklyn ran exhibits of his artwork, with plans to take them on to London, Berlin, and Tokyo. He began competing on an international level, challengers coming to him as wildlife travel restrictions proved too complicated for William to risk venturing abroad. Plus he enjoyed staying put in his hometown, spending days on the grass and nights in his studio.

It takes a special type of badminton player to want to go up against an avian swarm. Countless contenders adopted bizarre training regimens in the hopes of becoming the one to finally beat William Wegmuller and his flock. Meditating for long hours at the tops of trees. Having hundreds of birdies hit at them simultaneously, the main one remaining white, while the rest had been dyed to match a plethora of plumage patterns. Wrapping themselves in worms and walking otherwise naked through local sanctuaries. But once face to face with William, even those who had distinguished themselves through such maniacal methods came up short. Quite a few arrived armed with duck calls, shown to be merely noisemakers, as no water fowl ever rose to their aid. One particularly nefarious adversary whisked their way onto the court dressed in a cloak and more sinister version of William's hat, terrifying symbols sketched upon its brim, but this fellow was promptly banned for attempting to use a spiked racket. Lance Hardaway even took a break from his own rise on the California badminton circuit to train a woodpecker to fly in and snag the shuttle mid-air, a highly controversial move which was nevertheless thwarted when the red-breasted sapsucker ended up joining William's entourage after the 12th point.

A most curious occurrence came to overshadow all of these. One afternoon when William was due to stop in at the Philadelphia gallery, a woodcock appeared at his beard, captivating its residents. The seven soon followed this visitor up into the air, mimicking its magnificent sky dance. William, pressed for time, was forced to leave for the city without his usual entourage, repeatedly checking mirrors as the difference in weight dangling from his chin gave him the peculiar sensation of being freshly shaven. It was only hours after William had come back home, eaten dinner, and was finishing a new painting, that the eight returned, elated and chirping long into the night.

By now, being so in demand on the international art and badminton scenes, William often lost track of who he was up against next, choosing to focus on his own performance rather than the ragtag bags of tricks that passed for the latest slew of challengers to his title. But when Wilhelmina Woodhouse sashayed up to the net two days later, he wished he had been paying more attention, his beard now positively abuzz. Their eyes locked and, the game yet to begin, it was love at first sight.

Still, this was a competitive match that a lot of people had paid good money to see. The two shook hands, lingering just long enough before Wilhelmina strode back and fired off the first serve. William admired her power, returning it in kind. This went on for some time, though with each stroke the players inched, almost imperceptibly, closer and closer to the center line. The set collapsed into a volley of hairpin shots, their thin arcs describing countless W's, William and Wilhelmina's initials over and over again approaching eternity. The spectators were mesmerized by the electricity coming off the court but William and Wilhelmina's desire to touch one another again could not be delayed forever. With their excellent sense of showbiz timing, the swallows, swifts, thrushes, orioles, bluebirds, and even hawks of the area swooped in from the wings, thousands this time, more than had ever been witnessed before, circling and circling at greater speed, obscuring the two soon-to-be lovers and giving them a safe space, while the crowd marveled at the carousel of color spinning before their eyes.

William and Wilhelmina married that December, their nuptials kicking off The Twelve Days of Christmas. Smokey and Bandit carried in Wilhelmina's ring, balanced lovingly between their beaks as they fluttered down the aisle. Frog and Snowman did the same for William's. Robinson, Port, and Starbird lifted Wilhelmina's train as she sauntered to the altar placed at center court. The woodcock, now named 'Woody', sat perched on the attending minister's left shoulder. On New Year's Eve, the couple left to honeymoon at Lance Hardaway's guest cottage in Bodega Bay, California, the birds graciously departing William's beard for the night.

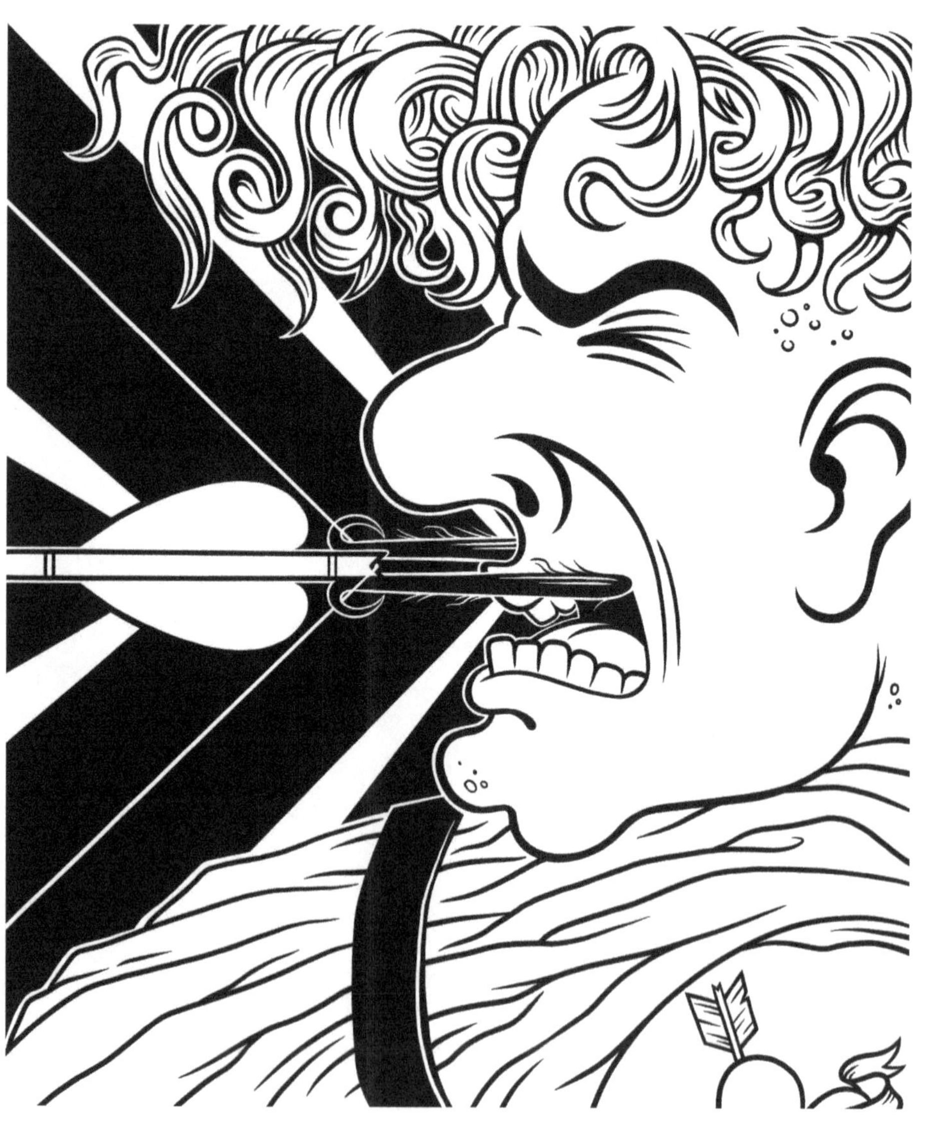

DATING PRETEXT

DEREK "BO" BEAUMAN'S fate seemed decreed by his last name. Indeed, the family had been known as Archer until a quite unfortunate mishap necessitated a change. Decades before the days of texting, when the idea of the telephone was still ringing throughout the ether and long before Alexander Graham Bell decided to answer it, Errol Archer ran his own rather unique communications service. While modern drama mostly seems to spring forth from nothingness—sinisterly arranged letters and overwrought emojis appearing where seconds ago there had only been blank space—back in the 17th and 18th centuries, even the delivery of such histrionics possessed real flair. Capitalizing on the skill that had bestowed upon the clan their surname, young Errol found early success in transmitting messages over great distances quicker than any postal system going could do the same. His method, of course, being the bow and arrow, and he called his fledgling company FLINT. Whilst in his more romantic moods, spending much of the day as he did copying down poetry from pining sweethearts, he would wax acrostic that the moniker stood for Flying Love In Noteworthy Texts or Flinging Letters Into New

Territories, the word FLINT was simply taken from the material from which the tools of his trade were made.

Focusing in as he would upon a target, Errol refined his business model to a subscription service for the young people looking to allay their insecurities by coupling up. Renting notice boards in all the main squares of the neighboring towns in his little corner of England, for a small fee one could offer a description of oneself and even include an artist's rendering of one's features if so inclined. Then, based on these depictions, if an interested party wanted to correspond with or even meet you, they could pay extra to let you know via Errol. He even styled his bounteous black beard, tapering it to end in a sharp point right above his heart, so that taken as a whole it appeared to be a wide arrow descending from mouth into the organ of love, thus becoming a walking advert for his trade, connecting man and means in the public mind.

Business was soon booming, behooving him to buy a horse, duly christened Caberneigh, and life became a constant circuit of the 20 or so miles they regularly covered, sleeping when he could, often for only an hour or two, and switching up his trajectory depending on the cash paid out by the most impatient of suitors. Errol charged by the word, the distance, and the timeframe. Often he would be sent ahead for a party already set out, to thwack into the beloved's wall a scroll, upon which the details for that evening's rendezvous would unfurl. And it was during just such a routine assignment that the incident would occur that would devastate his livelihood and force him to flee country forever.

Young Joan Burroughs was already waiting for him that fine spring morning when he rode into Matchingham, tying

Caberneigh to his usual post. She had written out her message herself, or rather, with her usual panache, had sliced the words that expressed her innermost desires out of newspapers, town notices, and previously discarded FLINT communiqués, then lacquered the phrases onto parchment, rolling this up to hand over to Errol along with her payment. The final recipient of this missive was to be one Graham Tell, whom she had met two days before whilst visiting the village of Bumbleborough, some miles away.

Errol knew Tell well, and in fact was expecting Graham to have some dispatches of his own to send out today, not to Joan but another young lass with whom he was recently acquainted and had been exchanging love letters like a lightning storm. Descending from his horse onto the low hill just above the village gate, as luck would have it, Errol spied Tell walking through the market and stopping to purchase a plump red apple. Though it was not his usual way, Archer decided to have a little fun with his friend. He readied his bow, watching as Tell shined the fruit on the front of his shirt, bringing it up to his mouth to chomp down. As Tell removed the sphere from his lips, Errol fired. Now, Archer's accuracy could never be in question, he was the best shot in the land. It was a direct hit, the arrowhead exploding through the apple's core to lodge itself in the wall behind, unfurling Joan's message right before Graham's eyes. With which he would have read the hanging text were it not for the commotion startling him enough to choke on the bite of said apple that he had not yet finished chewing. Phoebe Butler, who had been on her way to join him in his perambulations, screamed as she saw Graham double over, unable to breathe, not four steps ahead of her. She ran, grabbing

Graham from behind, ramming her fists into his chest until he spewed out the half-masticated fruit. As he stood up to resume respiration, Phoebe, having had time to be affronted by the jarring fonts of this letter from another woman, smacked Graham across the face and made to storm off. Her progress prevented by a rather large pig, who, out for a walk with its owner, had spied the remains of the apple on the ground and made a beeline for it, tripping up Phoebe as she turned to fall flat on her face. A face that, having descended upon precious pieces of produce, the pig began nudging out of the way with its snout and tongue.

Riled up by the sight of a woman in such a misconstrued display with a pig as well as by Tell's garbled shouts of intended revenge, an angry mob bolted out the gate. They knew who they were looking for, it could only be one man. Errol made it to Caberneigh just in time, hopping into the saddle as desperate fists arced through the air. He kicked his heels in and the two galloped to safety, but not before hearing his bow string snap, the blade of the sword responsible missing his left arm by millimeters.

The local, less aerodynamic, press had a field day as lawsuits were brought against Archer from Tell, Butler, and the proprietor of the pig. Errol was being sued for damages to account for Phoebe's defamation, distress, and destroyed dress. Graham sought to use the opportunity to place himself as the victim and thus reverse all the nasty little predicaments that were popping up concerning his multitudinous affairs. A nice sum of money would greatly help as a disinfectant to his besmudged name. Plus the cost of the apple. And having not procured the pig's snack himself, its keeper was most outraged as to what consequences might befall the animal's digestive tract in the long term. Errol's 'straight as an arrow' reputation was in ruins. Truth be told, the newspapers, envious of the business taken away from their classified listings, had been waiting for something like this to happen. They did not miss a chance to smear Archer's character with conjecture over what this madman might do next. Attempt to light Old Man Chapman's pipe with flying flames? Kill someone with their own death notice? Harpoon a blueberry? Parents outright banned their children from using Archer's services and, as Graham could almost always be found describing to a small crowd the lingering pain in his apple-holding hand, young men became wary of what other body parts Errol might take aim at.

Hiding out in the hills he knew so well, having already abandoned Caberneigh to her fate, after some days Errol made his way quick-as-he-could on foot for Southampton, stopping on his first night to snip off his telltale beard. He could not, however, bring himself to part with it, and on the transatlantic voyage which eventually brought him to Hingham, Massachusetts, Errol used his glorious locks to restring his bow. But upon settling on these shores, he thought it best to give up his former life and stash said stick in the attic of his new home. He adopted the surname 'Beauman', its connotations of 'good man' bolstering his ego after the bashing it had recently undergone, not bothering to correct the many who chose to believe he came from France, a most convenient decoy, and, as he had always carved his own bows, soon took up the occupation of furniture making.

Errol never spoke of the incident again and went to his grave wondering what became of Graham Tell, Phoebe Butler, and Joan Burroughs. He would see his many grandchildren grow up but not any of their progeny, amongst whom, in 1904, Derek was born. The boy was the younger son of Mark Beauman, who had inherited the contents of his grandfather's attic, now transferred to his own. And it was here one day in 1907, that Derek came across the object for which he would become known far and wide. Quite literally. The nickname deriving from 'Beauman' would naturally have fallen to the eldest child, Sebastian, but it was Derek who found the carved yew first, giving him a sense of destiny. He came running downstairs, plucking its string that no one would have guessed was made of ancestral hair, and to the resonating pitch of its low A, asked his father what this was. Mark smiled, "That's called a bow." Derek repeated the word until he became identified with it. 'Bo Beauman', like a heartbeat that was to fuel his life.

He was already quite the archer by the time he reached puberty, winning local and then state competitions. When the first hairs began to appear on his upper lip, much like those sprouting elsewhere, he encouraged their growth. Every now and then he thought he could feel them being willed through his skin by a force outside himself. And when finally this tasche hung below his chin, he did not question the hand that automatically pulled those strands into his grip as he took aim. When the hair on his face came into contact with the drawstring of the bow like this, Bo felt an almost psychic connection that he could not explain. He simply had to visualize his shot, let the shaft fly, and it ended up where it should. Upon this discovery, he strode coolly back into the house, grabbed three apples from the bowl on the kitchen table, and asked his brother Sebastian to join him outside. He positioned Sebastian against a tree, placed two of the pieces of fruit, one atop the other, on his brother's head, and, tossing the third to Sebastian to hold, walked back 100 paces. Sebastian stood patient as a saint as Bo then spent the following few minutes in silent contemplation. The older sibling wasn't nervous, Bo had performed this trick before. But what happened next wasn't like anything Sebastian had previously experienced. Bo raised his instrument, took moustache betwixt fingers as he pulled back the string, closed his eyes in concentration, and let go. The arrow swooped to his right, came down to kiss the ground before ascending back towards the target, knocking the top apple clear off Sebastian's head as it cruised past at 90 degrees straight over his left ear. Before Sebastian could close his shocked mouth, the other fruit fell from a parallel projectile on the opposite side.

Bo smiled, calling to his brother, "Put the last one on your head", and Sebastian, dumbstruck, did as requested. During stunts like these, Sebastian had always adopted a wide-legged stance, the better to balance and brace himself against the oncoming force. He dug in, quite thrown by the impossibilities of what his brother had just unleashed. And there was still one more surprise in store.

Sebastian felt the familiar flush of fear that comes from seeing a fragment of flint flying full speed towards your forehead. Only this one, at about 15 feet away, dipped down lower. Sebastian clenched his eyes shut, breath and motion ceasing as he knew the slightest shuffle could grievously interfere with his brother's expert marksmanship. A very real shiver shot up his spine as the arrow split the tree inches above and between his now shaking kneecaps. Over a hundred feet away, Bo doubled over in hysterical laughter. He calmly walked up to his brother, snatching the apple from his head. And then, for reasons he could not explain, rubbed it the length of his drawstring before chomping into his first bite.

Bo soon retired from competitions, preferring to indulge this newfound theatricality in a series of touring carnival acts, becoming famous enough to warrant his own Derek Beauman Tent. He bought a home in the suburbs of Boston and whenever he was in town, he would often take to the Common to put on displays of his most recent array of dazzling arcs, loop-de-loops, and other assorted tricks. One day as he was setting up for such a performance, as he took his tasche into his hand to shoot, a vision came to him, seemingly from out of nowhere. Burning bright in his mind's eye, Cupid merrily made his way through a vast woods, drawing undecipherable hieroglyphs in the sky with the tips of his trade as he strode along. When Bo took his hand off the drawstring, the image faded as quickly as it had come.

At the end of the exhibition, after all the fans seeking autographs and would-be Robin Hoods looking to talk shop began to make their ways home, Bo spied a morose-looking young man sitting on a park bench sketching something quite intensely. Heading over to the youth, Bo noticed that the lines on the page bore a striking resemblance to a young woman whom had not ten minutes ago been lavishing adoration on Bo himself. "Didn't you enjoy the show?" Bo queried. "Yes, but . . ." and the young man nodded towards the rendering of the woman's face. "I see," came Bo's reply as the palm holding his equipment unconsciously rose to stroke his moustache in a pantomime of ponderous thought. As hair again connected with hair, another idea that seemed to come from beyond struck him. Quickly he snatched the sheet of paper from the boy, attached it with some resin to a shaft, and fired in the direction he had seen the young woman and her friends depart. Guided by who knows what, the missile smacked into the Park Street elm tree she was just about to pass, the parchment unfolding down to reveal her own likeness before her very eyes. The woman, quite rightly, ran.

The following day Bo received a letter from his father asking if he would like his great-grandfather's writing desk for his new home. Bo sensed that he should accept this offer. Despite the outcome of his matchmaking attempt yesterday, the vision of Cupid sashaying through the woods would not leave him alone and he discerned there was something to both messenger and method. This he felt all the more keenly whenever he held up his bow. The forest aspect appeared important, for what else do trees produce besides bows and arrows but paper?

He set to work, commissioning a custom Cupid costume, believing such an outfit would lend a certain weight to his activities. Bo reasoned that, once they were aware of his presence, which was nothing a little advertising wouldn't take care of, people would be more apt to accept an eccentrically-dressed figure firing off scrolls seemingly willy-nilly than a regular-looking stranger operating in the same manner. To highlight the fact that his missives were to be of the amorous variety, he settled on the company name Bo Kommunications, to be known as BO K, and meant to evoke romantic arrangements, floral and otherwise. For an extra sum, he would even weave rose, tulip, and orchid petals into the parchment.

It took somewhat longer for Bo to get business off the ground than it had for his great-grandfather, Errol. Bo's services did not come cheap and people weren't all that keen on having any sort of object unsuspectingly stream through their third-story windows, even if it was by a man in the garb of a mythological being. Once things picked up, however, receiving a BO K became something of a status symbol. Bo's initial hunches that what he offered would mostly appeal to the new generation proved correct. Regardless of what others might later claim, Boston was indeed a big college town, and its curfews were the bane of young lovers. Students partially allayed their frustrations by employing Bo to convey uncensored communiqués from campus to campus.

Shortly after the New Year of 1929, having spent the holiday season accepting insane long-distance challenges from those estranged over the Christmas break, Bo finally began to break through. True, his train fare, which the customer covered anyway, did not reflect the actual degree of separation, as his talent allowed him to disembark stations ahead of his target and still deliver with astounding accuracy, saving himself hours in the process. With the students back after their recess, he was steadily engaged—making dates, propelling proposals, and even occasionally hired to send up fireworks high over the dirty waters of the Charles River to the delight of couples who had come together through his efforts. But Boston winters are cold, even dropping to 6 degrees Fahrenheit that January. An asinine time to be out dressed in only a loincloth and large pair of fake wings. Nevertheless, stopping now might be career suicide. Especially with the holiday he was made for coming up the following month.

Well-informed archers with their noses to the ground will always find some sort of work on Valentine's Day. Though, like with anything else, 'true artists' of the craft, with their own nostrils in the air, will be heard railing against the commerciality of the occasion, often as they are accepting a drink from a fellow bowsman who has no such qualms about earning his bacon by taking advantage of the situation. And on this date in 1929, Derek 'Bo' Beauman was scheduled to bestow good fortune upon Patricia Handelman and Skippy Hertz as they took their matrimonial vows, firing the rings at giant wooden hearts arranged either side of the altar at the climax of the ceremony. It was freezing out as Bo made his way from his home in Jamaica Plain to the chapel in Somerville across the Charles. Whereas this job usually kept him in the open air, tonight he found himself ducking into a garage to hire a taxi for the journey.

After arranging the fare, before Bo could take even one step towards his awaiting vehicle, a shop door opened causing him to stiffen. The hairs on the back of his neck as well as those running the entire length of his bow stood on end, all aquiver. As he turned to face the entryway, he was thrown back with great force by two simultaneous shots, arrowheads piercing his moustache tips straight back through his wings and smack into the wall behind.

"Can't fly away now, archer."

A darkly clad duo emerged from the shadows, their faces hidden underneath wide hat brims, chewing cigar stubs in unison. They introduced themselves as working for the firm of Martin & Murphy, hired by the descendants of Graham & Phoebe Tell, née Butler, to exact what was owed their family.

Bo, squirming against the wall, had no idea what they were talking about. The heavies continued on, explaining the whole sordid story—the great offence Errol Archer had caused on that distant day, how the tale had been told and retold throughout the Tell lineage, and how after decades of sitting with the case, Martin & Murphy finally caught wind of a lead via reports of Bo's aerodynamic antics from circus-loving tourists recently returned home to England. Having listened, Bo instantly knew, felt even at the deepest level, that his drawstring was made of his great-grandfather's hair, and that his choice of occupation had been ordained long before he came into this world.

"What is it you want? Money?"

"It's too late for that, Mr. Beauman. What is required now is justice."

And with that, one goon seized his right hand while the other produced an unreasonably large knife and removed Bo's bow finger.

Quickly as they had come, the thugs disappeared out into the night, leaving Bo's gear scattered on the floor behind him. For although they were hired hoodlums, they understood the importance of family. A head poked above a desk beneath which the owner of the garage had been hiding and the man rushed to set Bo free. With little time to spare, the two cauterized Bo's wound, and, grabbing a whisky bottle for the pain, set off at speed for the wedding. Bo's mind was also racing. He had worked so hard to build up his business, he couldn't back out now. But how was he to aim effectively with his hand so off-balance? And his whole body more than a little tipsy. There would be no room for error in the tight quarters of the church. Yet he had to try. From what the two fiends had told him, he was more certain than ever of his destiny. Upon arrival, he secured the wedding bands, raised his bow with a sense of all its newly revealed history, and took his tasche under his formerly middle finger. The connection calmed him. He envisioned where the rings must land and let fly. With such damage to hand and spirit, the arrow's path was not as streamlined as Bo would've liked. But the course of true love itself never runs smooth, and despite encountering many obstacles of their own, Patricia and Skippy are still together today.

An Early History Of The Three-Faced Race

LOCAL FLÂNEURS Puffy Pullman and Cheeks Redborne lay in the grass under the cool shade of an oak tree as the 1972 Summer Solstice stretched through 3 p.m. and the festivities of the Harrisonburg Summer Fair showed no signs of abating. They had been drinking red wine since the cock crowed the morning, for while they never participated in the town's activities, they relished the fête as an excuse for making merry, believing their witty commentary on all things Harrisonburg to reach its peak just as year ascended to its own. They were quite drunk by now, their long moustaches stained various shades of burgundy from the myriad bottles scattered about their matching custom leather shoes. While they took pride in their appearance, for both were well-dressed in floral pattern collared shirts under dark suit jackets, even donning capes for this most special event, the same care could not be said of the attitude pertaining to their physiques. Their already far-from-athletic builds were running to mush, exacerbated by the switch to the legal side of being able to purchase alcohol, both having turned 18 the previous autumn. This they did plenty of, believing themselves, in some respects correctly, to be bon vivants, and now that the weather was more copacetic they relished relishing the good life out in it. Cheeks was letting loose a torrent of guffaws at the proceedings on the field while Puffy had his face buried in the crook of his arm, giving him, if not for the presence of the Sun, a most vampire-like appearance, having had to avert his eyes due to an overdose of hilarity some moments before. The two were watching the annual three-legged race.

Its victors, Joseph Flockhart aka Joe Flow and Frasier Price, often called 'Mr. Right', a nickname encompassing much more than his relative position to his running partner, showed little pride in having won the competition as they made their way over to the long grass to confront, with accumulated aggravation from many years of dealing with the same, the rebellious duo rolling about hysterically within.

"You might come to appreciate how funny it really is if you were out there yourselves, instead of giggling like cowards at those of us who actually compete."

Puffy jumped to his feet, landing unsteadily but still impressively for a man who'd drank three bottles of wine since breakfast, which itself had been another bottle of wine. "No one calls Puffy Pullman a coward! We will race you, sir, with our beautiful moustaches tied together!"

Cheeks unconsciously grimaced, rubbing his face in anticipation, for he was the taller of the two, by three inches. But he always had Puffy's back, using this now to hoist himself up to a standing position in order to modify his cohort's challenge.

"You gentlemen must be tired after having just run such a race, albeit a lightweight version thereof. We wouldn't want to put you in the disadvantageous position of us having legs all the fresher." He hiccupped to emphasize what, in his advanced state of inebriation, he considered a point well made.

Joe Flow smirked. "Any time, any place. Just name it."

Puffy swayed again before stomping to keep himself upright. Whatever the reason, it provided purposeful punctuation to his pronouncement. "Tomorrow, here, at dawn!" He wobbled then stamped out a final, "And by that we mean 1 p.m."

Joe and Frasier also smoothed their palms over their chins, in a much-less-masochistic manner than Cheeks had done a moment ago. By no means clean-shaven, their affected stubble wasn't lengthy enough to tie to anything, but that had not been part of the deal as stated. It was their turn to chuckle. "One p.m. then" and they moved off back into the crowd.

Cheeks and Puffy drank long into the night, at first expounding on the geniusness of their idea and how easily they would win, the world being their hairy oysters. Then of course as drinking sessions are wont to proceed, they would forget all about it, returning to the plan hours later with renewed enthusiasm. They talked and talked and talked and talked, often breaking out into spontaneous sprints, to then, amidst desperate gasps and frequent clenchings of eyes and fists, congratulate the other on a race already won, bestowing further felicitations for their incredible courage, creativity, and fortitude. They didn't go as far as actually trying to tie their moustaches together though, for each secretly thought this was insane.

When they arrived at the field the next day at 1:15, very hungover and still in yesterday's clothes though sporting different, bluer, capes, Puffy and Cheeks were surprised to see the area as full as the day before. They had assumed, secretly hoped to some extent, that no one would show and they could go back to bed without having to make good on their challenge. Each removed their sunglasses to look the other in the eye, marveling at how the news had traveled concerning their bold attempt to revolutionize racing as the world knew it, though the crowd, in their own words, was gathered to 'watch the degenerates make complete fools of themselves'. Nevertheless, local beauty Lacey Locke, on whom Cheeks had harbored a secret crush since the second grade, offered to tie their moustaches for them. Even as the slight tugs suggested otherwise, this seemed to them a good omen. Though it was only now they realized, that despite Cheeks' proclamation of yesterday, they would be the ones at a disadvantage as Joe Flow and Mr. Right had no true facial hair to speak of, let alone do anything with.

Seeing this comprehension dawning in their eyes, Mr. Right stepped forward. "Tell ya what, fellas, to make things more fair, I'm gonna race on the left today."

The contestants lined up for what was to be a 100 meter dash. The ten paces to starting positions proved to be an unending path of pain and confusion for Pullman and Redborne. Cheeks feeling the strain all the more as he was hunched over to level himself with Puffy's face. He longed for Lacey's caressing hands, though asking her to tighten the already uncomfortable knot was out of the question. His mind frantically searched for other options. Simultaneously, a solution struck the pair as for a brief moment the copious clouds of hangover were pierced by the shining light of logic. Puffy and Cheeks hissed through tight teeth, "Our legs shall be bound together as well!"

The crowd gasped. Joe offered, "You guys don't have to do that—" but Puffy cut him off.

"We will not make a mockery of . . . the three-legged race . . . by not . . . running on . . . three . . . legs!" Wincing at every ellipsis. It only now dawning on him how many muscles are involved in speaking, as they spasmed with each movement of the jaw. Resolving to keep this to a minimum.

His real motive for tethering their lower limbs he kept secret. That even in those first tentative steps he could tell having an anchor would greatly aid them, preventing their torsos from straying too far, and thereby mitigating the torture that lay ahead, each footfall a serpent's tail upon which it was impossible not to tread. Cheeks silently yet whole-heartedly agreeing.

The starter pistol fired and it felt as if real bullets pierced straight through their eardrums. They weren't past the hangovers yet. Price and Flow hopped along three meters and then turned to see how their challengers were making out, an apt way of putting it as Puffy and Cheek's lips met at the corners. Their feet, however, had not left the starting line. And any comments about them kissing were held at bay by the fear in their eyes. Lacey Locke and other less voluptuous spectators offered words of advice and encouragement. The important thing was not to fall. Everyone sensed this implicitly. The pain sure to be engendered should they topple over, hair pulled past the limits of what any human could bear, made the additional risk of heads cracking into unconsciousness, no matter what injuries sustained thereafter, seem like blessed relief. It was vital to keep their cheeks pressed against each other, as hard as they could, the same going for thighs, calves, and ankles, to maintain as narrow a stride as possible. "Start with your middle legs," Lacey intoned mischievously, and with a slight push sent them on their way. Her extra touch was heavenly anodyne for Cheeks, and it was another few seconds before he joined in on harmony to Puffy's ode to whimpering.

By the time the two of them worked up an awkward momentum, Joe Flow and Frasier Price had completed the course, facing backwards the whole way, fully luxuriating in their victory, and were now returning at speed to watch the proceedings more closely. That they themselves had lost within half a minute of beginning never registered with Puffy and Cheeks, so great was their concentration elsewhere. Still having 95 meters to cover, hungover and sweating out alcohol and fear in the summer heat, things looked bleak, and efforts to discuss the matter were complicated by how much it hurt to move their mouths. After many thwarted attempts, Puffy alighted upon the solution to communicate telepathically. A no-brainer given both the circumstances and proximity of those particular organs. His initial suggestion of which, also sent via his mind, went unanswered by Cheeks, who was at the same time trying to, with the full force of *his* grey matter, mystically message Lacey to come to their aide again. Incensed that his ethereal extrusions were somehow going unheeded, Puffy railed out loud against his comrade "Focus!" But even this command was lost as the two grit their teeth, agonized by the utterance and its ensuing muscular reverberations.

Until now the crowd had been unusually quiet, a few hoots of support here and there but most wordlessly watching in wait for what might happen. This pregnant silence was burst by a shout of "quit your whining and get on with it!"

Cheeks and Puffy's eyes lit up like a power surge, and reflexively each attempted to look at the other, turning only so far as the strain on their faces would let them. They had been given a solution, it was just a matter of voicing it.

"Wine!" they cried in unison, striving to get the sounds out with a minimum of brutal repercussions. The crowd, startlingly, let the plea pass as if they hadn't heard. A panic that could not be easily conveyed as separate from their overall predicament entered Puffy and Cheeks' collective countenance. After so much exertion, excruciating they might add if each articulated syllable wasn't just that, they had finally realized what they needed and broadcast it at great expense, to now have no one understand them, or care to. Dancing about as best they could, the two learned the hard way that there really is no effective pantomime for the word 'wine' when you're tied to another human being by face, thigh, and ankle. Eventually that sweet angel Lacey grasped what they were trying to convey, and like the wonder that she is, was soon bounding towards them with a jug in her hands. Causing a whole other set of difficulties to arise. If moving their mouths to speak was this problematic, how were they going to open them to sup the desired nectar? But there was no time to plan. Lacey held the bottle over their conjoined faces and poured, the two lapping it up like dogs, each other's swallows a high but welcome price to pay for such sweet relief. It soon became apparent that they would not be able to imbibe enough to kill the pain, and, truth be told, drinking under these conditions made them feel slightly sick, but the first, thankfully repressed, spasms of vomit that they felt reaching up from the other's torso was something they actually did telepathically agree to never mention again.

They were still a good 70 meters from the finish line but peculiar sensations began to come over them. They had passed a hurdle, metaphorically of course, as jumping in their current circumstances would surely bring about the end of their sanity. Soon the words of the poets and philosophers rose from their literary memories to ring rapturously in their ears—Nietzsche, Goethe, Sartre, and others whose surnames did not end in 'uh'. A confidence that was difficult to differentiate from madness descended upon the pair. They began to believe they could do it. Wild-eyed, they hit a stride, Cheeks drumming out the rhythm on Puffy's shoulder—three light taps, then a more forceful hit signaling the forward thrust on their middle legs. Tears of anguish mixed with those of joy, an elation that radiated out through the crowd, who were now fully on their side, cheering them on. The vision of Lacey blowing Cheeks a kiss with 30 yards left to go was one he would take unto his grave.

The ribbon across the finish line was quickly reinstated to mark just how big a deal their crossing it would be. They did so looking like two men possessed, and with the inhabiting demons trying to punch their way out from the center of their skulls. Vast amounts of sweat poured over skin stained red with sunburn and wine, creased deep from endless suffering endured. The impression that they were lunatics was not helped by their repeated shouts of 'Scissors!' as they stumbled the final few meters, grimacing at the torment brought about by expressing such requests. It took a moment for the spectators to see that the knot between their tasches was taut beyond hope of loosening. The mayor, always something of a jokester, pushed his way to the front holding the outsized pair of shears he used for ceremonial openings and the like. Cheeks nearly lost consciousness when he saw Lacey remove them from the old man's hand and begin to approach bearing the widest, prettiest smile he'd ever seen. When the snip was made, the friends fell away from each other, tumbling to the ground, Cheeks landing at Lacey's feet, Puffy vomiting profusely into his cape. But despite the awful smell escalating rumblings deep within him, there was no way Cheeks was going to let himself follow suit. For above were a pair of lips awaiting his. The official with the stopwatch noted that this occurred a good 33 minutes after Joe Flow and Mr. Right had already achieved victory. But the winners were magnanimous, even coming up to shake hands. Well, Cheeks' hand. And to Puffy, "We didn't think you had it in you."

That summer the boys enjoyed local celebrity status, relishing the attention the townsfolk lavished. No longer was it just the two of them in the shadowy overgrown grass with a few bottles of vino. The town's youth, disaffected and otherwise, gathered to hear Puffy pontificate, whilst Cheeks and Lacey made out behind the bushes a few yards away.

The following year, however, Harrisonburg would not be graced with their presence, the two having discovered the charms of the big city where both had moved to attend college at the end of that last glorious August. But the memory of the race—now muddled by time to be believed to have taken part on the Solstice itself—lingered on, the fair's main topic of conversation as those in attendance scanned the boundary lines for a much hoped-for glimpse of Puffy and Cheeks' return.

A curious thing then happened in 1983. Michael Shell, who had been five years old at the time what became known as 'The Three-Faced Race' took place, turned 16 that May and was in possession of quite the moustache himself. To anyone who knew the inner workings of Michael's mind this would come as no surprise, for back in '72 he, like most other Harrisonburg males of all ages, harbored the most hardcore crush on Lacey Locke. Seeing her actions on that day set in motion the course for his life. He began willing his facial hair into existence, and as soon as it sprouted, he tended to it as if he were training for a marathon. Shaving his upper lip, and, truth be told, any body hair that was poking through any surface at that point, as he had heard this would make it grow in thicker. Sending away for special ointments advertised in the back of his mother's magazines, always racing home from school to be sure he was the one to get the mail, lest his family divine his secret ambitions before their time. And when the hair really started to come in, pulling on it for hours a day to get the strands further past the barrier of the skin and out into full view. Nevermind that Lacey Locke had moved to the city and married Cheeks Redborne years ago. That Van Halen came into his life soon after their nuptials greatly helped to ease the heartache. There were other Harrisonburg girls to impress, closer to his age, particularly the delectable Donna Teller.

Although there had been plenty of recent occasions where Miss Teller had glanced his way, said hi in the school halls, even whispering to her best friend she would go to the spring dance with him if he asked, tempting as these opportunities were, Michael ignored them. No, if she were the one, he would win her over on the hair-tied-and-true battlefield in the same way his hero/rival had done with the gorgeous Miss Locke. He refused to consider any other plotline to this ideal love story. And Michael had big plans. He spent months constantly dropping hints until his best friends Angelo Hanger, Leo Jupitus, and Raf Scallion agreed to start growing their facial hair too. That it just so happened Michael and Angelo were each 5 feet 8 inches tall, while Leo and Raf both measured in at an even six feet, Michael took as proof that his ambitions were meant to be.

Laying out his vision for the four friends, Michael then waited strategically until late May to approach the town recreational committee. The officials agreed to host a special exhibition revival of The Three-Faced Race in honor of Puffy Pullman and Cheeks Redborne, whose band The Low Brows were now enjoying the fruits of new wave success. Invitations were sent to the rock stars and all hoped they would make the trip back to Harrisonburg. Meanwhile, with less than a month to go until the fair, Michael Shell's tactics were working. Although the event would be open to all, he knew of no other local men with moustaches substantial enough to participate. To be sure, he continued to delay the announcement, though finally, with the Solstice being only a week away, he could hold off the news no longer. In the interim, the quartet had trained as they had all year. Knowing it could very well be the end of their moustaches if they attempted to tie them ahead of time, they were saving that key ingredient until the big day, instead running drills in Michael's secluded back yard, one large sweatband stretched around each set of cheeks, pressing them together to simulate the real thing, with ankles and thighs bound as well.

All was running smoothly until, with three days to go, Michael's enthusiasm got the better of him, and in the spirit of camaraderie confessed to his teammates his true reasons behind the whole enterprise. He immediately regretted it. Angelo and Raf, resting against a nearby tree, drew their knees in close, looking awkwardly off into the distance as Leo stared Michael straight in the eye.

"You're interested in Donna? *I* like Donna."

No one knew what to say after that. The next day Leo did not show up to practice. Michael, though furious, was resolved that all should still run according to plan. They would race, he would win, and thus win Donna's heart. Nevermind that Donna had never expressed an interest in any of this, that too was just a minor bump in the road. Michael felt deep inside that there was no way she could not be mesmerized by his pulling off such a feat. He sent Raf to go talk to Leo. On the final night of practice, the eve of the fair, Leo arrived late with an ice-cold stare. The two suitors ceremoniously sat down at the Shell family table and decided that to the victor went all the spoils—Donna Teller, the first place trophy, the fame that Puffy and Cheeks had enjoyed, the subsequent possibility of them also going on to be in a famous pop band . . . They then went outside, attached themselves to their partners, and ran their asses off. Fate had provided a true kick in the pants, and Michael could not have orchestrated better inspiration himself.

Despite Michael's efforts to hold up the proceedings for his own nefarious purposes, Harrisonburg had wasted no time in getting word out about 'The Return Of The Three-Faced Race'. News spread that this time all parties involved would actually be bound by their facial hair, although once again it would be an event where the term 'three-faced' was questionable at best. An anticipatory crowd had gathered early at the gates, a large percentage carrying copies of The Low Brows' newly released 'Riding On The Handlebars (Of Love)' single, and all holding hopes that Puffy and Cheeks would show up to sign them. The number of local food vendors doubled since the previous year, awash with assortments of homemade goodies—cookies, cakes, and fruit arrangements depicting two faces joined by complex strands of frosting over the lips. The excitement was edible.

As the festivities began, Michael Shell, who, in contrast to his grand romantic visions, had always been rather shy around girls, came out of his carapace to walk right up to Donna Teller and ask her if she would do them the incredible honor of tying their moustaches together. Donna consented and agreed to meet the boys at the starting line. When the P.A. announced that enrollment for the Three-Faced Race was now open, Michael waited nervously near the sheet, eyeing every passerby like a G.I. Joe character at a ZZ Top concert, staring down anyone bearing the slightest hint of stubble. He breathed a huge sigh of relief when 3 o'clock came and there were only their four names written down, then walked towards the course with an overwhelming confidence that all would now run like clockwork. This was confirmed by the tingle shooting through his body when Donna's hands took hold of the end of his tasche. It had not occurred to him that she would also link Leo and Raf, but he was so wired that he let this pass. In doing so, he considered himself to be rather magnanimous, also knowing that it would deal an all-the-more crushing blow to Leo when in a few minutes time Michael left him in the dust.

The contestants took their places, arms around their partners, Leo staring daggers at Michael, with the latter pretending not to notice. The starter gun let rip and they were off. Those hoping to see a repeat of Puffy and Cheeks endearingly finding their way through a new world, harrumphing and hungover in the hot afternoon Sun, would be sorely disappointed. What the townsfolk of Harrisonburg now witnessed were two tri-legged well-oiled machines. Gone were the stops and uneasy starts, the eyes brimming with agony and anticipation of more, as well as all the whimpering. It was slow progress but steady, without even a pause for anyone to locate a bottle of wine. In fact, the only cries heard were at the finish line ten minutes later as Michael let out a resounding 'Yes!', Leo following two steps behind with an equally loud 'No!', and then all four letting loose with tormented shrieks brought about by those two ejaculations. Michael had little time to remain in pain, however, as his plan seemed to be working itself out right in front of his face. Donna Teller was making her way straight towards him, arms outstretched, a huge welcoming smile beaming from cheek to cheek. Michael closed his eyes to await the culmination of his dreams. A second later he felt a small section of Donna's lip on the corner of his, but something was definitely amiss. The rest of her physical presence was not where it should be. His lids shot open in spite of himself. It was now his turn to scream 'No!', long and loud, no matter how excruciating that was. Although his howl had been enough to interrupt Donna's tongue in Angelo's mouth, Michael yanked his head as well, cracking his partner's skull into his own. Leo and Raf, thankfully already cut free, dove into the mêlée along with a good number of spectators, grabbing Michael to restrain him from further headbutting Angelo, Leo taking the opportunity to deliver a few discreet blows to Donna's new beau. With four people holding Michael's head and another eight keeping his body still, the scissors finally made their way over to sever the two former best friends. Michael immediately stormed off the field, out of the fair, and back home as fast as he could.

When he arrived at the top of his driveway, smarting from ear to ear, both physically and spiritually, without fully knowing why, he threw open his mailbox. As he reached inside half-expecting another snake to take another bite out of his all-too-loving flesh, he froze when he saw what was there. Just as Lacey Locke's hands had first brought sweet relief to Cheeks Red borne on this very day (give or take 24 hours) over a decade ago, so now those same fingers gave much solace to one Michael Shell.

> *Dear Michael,*
>
> *We received your letter about reviving 'The Three-Faced Race' (how funny that it's called that now!) and Cheeks wanted me to write you that it's such a great idea! We both wish you the best of luck and wish we could be there, and would be, if The Low Brows weren't flying to Japan for their sold-out run of shows at Budokan that week. Maybe next year.*
>
> *Lots of Love,*
>
> *Lacey Locke Redborne*

In a way, it had all been worth it. Michael slept with this postcard under his pillow the entire lonely summer, and when school resumed that autumn he would often rush home for its balm after devastating days of seeing Donna passing notes to Angelo or the two holding hands in the hallway. The line 'maybe next year' reverberated in his head, and during Christmas break he began to notice more and more moustaches around town. On Valentine's Day, the date carefully chosen, Michael again petitioned the Harrisonburg committee about continuing The Three-Faced Race at the upcoming fair. Van Halen had released a new album, their best yet, and the sting of the previous event was gradually fading from his face and heart.

With the committee's approval, he set to work, opening up the competition county-wide, and of course sending another letter to Mr. & Mrs. Redborne well ahead of time. This year there would actually be three faces, as Leo and Raf would join Michael, leaning down the four inches either side of him, and the trio began training as soon as the snow thawed. On April 1st, word came in that The Low Brows would be honored to perform a special set the night of the Solstice, right in Harrisonburg. When the signed contract came back a week later, all let loose a huge sigh of relief that this wasn't an April Fool's joke. The big day came and meeting Lacey Locke was everything Michael Shell hoped it would be. The kiss she planted on his right cheek after he, Leo, and Raf won the race was a memory he too would take unto his grave. The trio came in at 11 minutes, not beating their previous time when each only had one partner to drag along, but it was a good showing nonetheless. Six other pairs from across the county had also signed up and all finished in under 15 minutes. Everyone was pleased with how the day went, and Puffy and Cheeks wandered about the grounds in amazement at how a spontaneous ejaculation twelve years before had grown into such a well-loved beast. They took the stage that evening with as much humility as their rock star egos would allow them and blazed through a set of their biggest hits—'Stiff Upper Lip', 'Tickle Tickle', and 'Yosemite Sam' from their *Red Hairing* album—encoring with a cover of David Bowie's 'Rubber Band' set to a disco beat. From its opening strains, the crowd went wild, and although most couldn't tell you what tune it was, all invaded the stage to dance with these triumphant sons of Harrisonburg.

By 1985, it was a foregone conclusion that the event would continue, as it was now the main feature of the fair. Michael Shell got planning early, hoping to expand the experience for spectators and competitors alike. There were some setbacks, the most obvious being David Lee Roth's departure from Van Halen, which Team Shell commemorated by wearing black arm bands, but when the day came it proved to be the most successful yet. The competition now consisted of ten groups of three, making it the first official 'Three-Faced Race', and Michael, Leo, and Raf set a record coming in at 9 minutes 27 seconds. Children shouted at the sidelines, waving Man-E-Faces and other He-Man action figures, dreaming dreams just like the young Michael Shell of one day joining the proceedings. Puffy and Cheeks both sent messages of congratulations, expressing both their love that the race was continuing and regrets that they could not make it this time around as their latest album, *Barbershop Bop*, was charting high in continental Europe, necessitating an onslaught of promotional appearances. But they would do their best for future fêtes.

And over the course of the years, Puffy, Cheeks, Lacey, and their families would all show up more often than not. Far after The Low Brows' fame began to fade, they were always welcome to perform a set in Harrisonburg, especially on the Solstice. And from such slow beginnings, the event has now been an annual occurrence for decades, where lifelong bonds have been forged simply by standing next to someone of similar height with a lengthy enough moustache. Indeed, three years ago there was an exhibition run of seventeen simultaneous faces, and visitors have traveled from Arnhem, NY and Bassett, CA to be part of the festivities. Michael, Leo, and Raf still hold the time to beat with 6 minutes 30 seconds in their last competitive run. And following a protracted on-again off-again relationship, Angelo Hanger and Donna Teller were finally married on the grounds in 1995. Michael Shell, still not technically speaking to the couple, made the arrangements, knowing that the special interest story would certainly draw in a larger crowd. Which it did. But to those who were there in 1972, even to Michael Shell, although it would severely pain him to admit it, there was a magic to that inaugural event, not so much a race as a willingness to make something happen, that all the later training and preparation could never recreate, not with a thousand linked moustaches blazing through the shadows of a summer field.

Cracking Up

THE ONLY THING Vincenzo Valentino, known to the world as 'Villoso', loved more than his initials was the water. He simply could not get enough of it. Swimming throughout the days of spring and summer, rowing when evening came, gleefully skating across when the season swayed and surfaces froze solid. Born and raised in Verona, he was well-placed to do so. His wealthy family wintered in the Italian Alps, vacationing further South amongst the Neapolitan shadows of Mount Vesuvius or near Malta's Grand Harbour in Valletta during the prime months of July and August. They also visited Venice at least once a year, where the Valentinos kept their own small fleet of personal gondolas. His favorite holiday spot, however, was Varna on the Bulgarian Riviera where he could frolic sunrise to sunset in the Black Sea. As his hair was the color of deepest night, he felt a special kinship with this body of water, where the word itself also started with a V in 'voda'.

He loved his hair also. And there was a lot to love. At the age of nine it had begun to sprout all over and never seemed to stop. By the time he turned sixteen in 1971, the world was more hirsute than it had been in decades, and, ever stylish, Villoso celebrated his birthday that May by shaving his chest into a V, proudly proclaiming who he was. This process would require repeating on a daily basis and he threw himself eagerly into its upkeep. All summer he would wrestle with the issue of this emblem's hydrodynamic impracticality, but instead of slowing him down in the water, as indeed any shaggy assemblage might, his vanity spurred him on as he pushed himself to compensate for the imposed lag, in the process developing an animal strength in his upper torso and legs that he wouldn't have otherwise. When the season ended and shirts found their way out of closets again, he let the practice go. Come All Saints' Day his body had returned to its natural bear-like state. While his family were visiting friends in Vermont that year, learning the customs of the American Thanksgiving holiday and sampling the vast array of snacks and carbonated beverages peculiar to that country, it occurred to Vincenzo that he could apply this concept in reverse to his cold weather pastimes. Unleashing the moustache he had been holding at bay, it soon formed its own inverted V extending down past his cheeks, rapidly making its way towards his shoulders. *Aero*dynamically, the wedge was promptly waxed and speeding him along, captivating all who saw him whirl across the ice, making short work of any would-be opponents. Vincenzo loved the way the air felt coursing over his face breakered by this chevron. By the end of November, he decided he was definitely keeping his *baffi*.

When spring rolled around and blades were put away in favor of hitting the beach, Villoso lost no time in shaving a fresh V above his ribs. On its first day back in full view, as he was strolling across the sands with his girlfriend Volpina, she took hold of the long bars drooping down from his lips and, producing a tube of petroleum jelly, fashioned them into form, noting with pleasure as she pulled them low enough to touch the tips of the V on his chest, how together they resembled a diamond. Villoso liked this very much. It symbolized the rarity of his athletic prowess, as well as his precision both on skates and amidst the waves. However, upon diving into the latter, the sharp points quickly dulled as strands unraveled and began to bulge outwards, rounding the whole shape. Volpina could not stop laughing when he emerged from the sea. "Tu sei l'uomo delle uova" she giggled, "you are the egg man." And, when she could finally catch her breath again, added "goo goo ga joob" before collapsing once more into hysterics. Villoso sighed, at least there was a V in 'uova'.

This new upper upside-down V actually made him an even better swimmer, its arrow deflecting water away from his frame, helping to propel him through the medium. The opposite was true of the V lower down. And as much as he loved his Superman-esque insignia, he did not want to become known as 'The Egg Man'. Amongst other things, it implicated a bone-chilling temporary status to the beautiful black locks that adorned his head. He took solace in the fact that at the rate his hair regenerated, he could sculpt the V whenever he felt like it, even performing topless on the ice if he so desired. Which he knew he often did.

From Vladivostok to Vancouver, Vilnius to Vail, Villoso indulged his passions, which increasingly now tended to be atop the water rather than within it. His confidence at a career high, he was concentrating on skating, both speed and figure, leaving little time for competitive swimming, and ignoring rowing completely. In a particularly inspired moment, Villoso hired a stylist, Vidal Bakun. Why not, he was making enough money from exhibitions and endorsements. He still insisted on shaving the V into his chest himself, a shamanic connection he was unwilling to forego, but Vidal was then called in to mirror the image onto Villoso's back. His seminude antics were gaining popularity, or at least he was frequently out on the ice that way, whenever, in fact, he was not outright banned from doing so. In his various dressing rooms, he would meticulously sharpen his moustache using the blade of his skate, and when the spotlight hit him as he took his place center ice, it indeed shone upon a perfect diamond. Two Vs, one flipped onto the other. His new trick, one which evoked a sense of wonder and sensation of razor burn, was to swan dive onto the surface and sail across, showing off his posterior V as he imagined his one below cutting into the rink, giving him progressively greater power with each embedded inch. After a long full body slide, he would push both himself and his moustache straight up into a Biellmann spin, the tip of his skate curled overhead and touching one end of his moustache, now flipped into a V-for-Victory. His routine finished, sure that he had dazzled the crowd, Villoso then danced back across the ice, kicking high to repeatedly connect toe to tasche.

All the applause and acclaim, the acknowledgement of his innovation and unique sense of style, was very appealing at first, but soon something began to vex Villoso. The feeling that he was ignoring a vital part of his great love of the water, that he wasn't getting as wet as he used to. This idea sometimes had a physical presence to it, and eventually it coalesced into a shape. An egg shape. His first sight of this apparition came in March of that year, towards the end of the 1974 season. Opening his Prague hotel room door after a particularly robust race down the frozen Vltava, from out of his peripheral vision he thought he espied a massive shimmering ovoid, its gloved hands gripping the corner as it peered around into his hallway from a face obscured by a wide-brimmed hat. He blinked and the image was gone. But not from his mind. A few days later as he was drifting off to sleep in Vaduz, he made the decision to travel to the Southern hemisphere and continue to work the competition circuit, effectively foregoing any chance of frolicking within the waves of the Mediterranean with Volpina that summer. The next morning over breakfast on his balcony, he heard a small voice say 'you could just as easily stay here until the autumn . . . and then head south for a more permanent summer'. Suspecting the words to be coming from inside his own head, they nevertheless seemed to exist in the space around him, his eyes a wild whirl, frantic to find their source. He saw nothing, of course. That is until he looked down into his bowl of cereal and specially imported root beer, another of his eccentricities, and he swore he saw a tiny egg, complete with face, arms, and legs, dangling its feet off the edge of a cornflake. The figure winked at Villoso, stood up and dove into the soda, a near perfect execution, disappearing under its dark bubbly surface with as little splash as its elliptical body would allow. Spooked, Villoso pushed the dish away, as well as, just to be safe, his Eggs Florentine.

This specter began to visit with increasing frequency, even following him to the other side of the globe, materializing most often when Villoso was in the shower or out walking in the rain. It seemed to be attempting to entice the skater back into the natural state of water and keep him there. During a storm in Vanderbijlpark, while rounding the corner to his lodgings, a van skidded past, Villoso catching a glimpse of its egg-shaped driver in full courier gear, wheels screeching as they sent up a giant cascade to utterly drench the Italian.

These sightings were rattling him, and more so than he believed. Becoming, although he refused to describe them in this way, a yoke around his neck. And lest they somehow weigh down his facial hair, Villoso took to waxing it up in a permanent V. This also being the peace sign, he found it convenient to tell the press it was his duty to display such a symbol as he travelled around the world, promoting international harmony whilst obscuring any inquiries they might have into his mental state. He did well bearing his secret, though he almost lost his cool when a journalist in Vanuatu, asking him about his choice of styling products, suggested that egg whites were also said to work wonders. By the time of his performance in Viedma, the star had unconsciously taken to stabbing his food with the tips of his moustache to then bend this spear back into his mouth, slurping off the morsels. Argentinian fans commenting that they'd be disgusted by the demonstration, if it weren't so fascinating. Having a rare afternoon off, Villoso wandered aimlessly, eventually happening upon a stream. Hoping to appease this haunting spirit, he rolled up his trouser legs, sat down on the bank, and let his feet hang free in the water. To be honest, it was a feeling he missed, and he let himself go, playing footsie with the algae. However, when he stood up to leave, a shock sent him right back down to his seat. Ascribing a rainbow-esque arc between two smokestacks in the distance was what appeared to be a gigantic flying pink egg. As it drew closer, Villoso couldn't help but stare in both fear and amazement. The object coming into sharper focus bore the face and ears of a pig. As this swine passed, it seemed to wink at the figure skater, who remained frozen to that spot for a good quarter of an hour.

Villoso felt the intense intent of this mystical entity stronger than ever now, and in another effort to placate it he booked two days in Virginia Beach before his next competition in Baltimore. Amidst all the swimming, diving, and general carousing in the brisk ocean, he actually began to relax and enjoy himself, though the egg demon was never far from the focal point of his mind. And sure enough when he boarded the midnight train to Maryland, coursing through the dark Virginia sky, right alongside his window sailed an oval raven, black as his own hair and backlit by the Moon. Villoso closed his eyes to blot out the sight, but to no avail as he quickly became haunted by visions of madmen from old black-and-white films tying a monstrous egg to the tracks using his moustache as the rope.

Despite being an honored guest at Vanda Station, Antarctica the following week, Villoso was ready to crack. Whenever he was left alone during the course of his three day stay, icy winds kicked up, heralding the arrival of an ellipsoidal penguin, pushing one of its enormous eggs towards him to boot, a shell that bore Villoso's own frozen face spinning round and round and round over the treacherous terrain. Greatly distressed, the skater holed up in his windowless room, dreading the continuation of his South American tour, especially the stop in Villavicencio slated for the end of the month.

It was here, in this lovely Colombian city that had seemed to call to him by name as it drew ever closer, that Villoso reached breaking point. As the otherwise largely favorable reviews highlighted, his routine that evening contained a record number of elongated figure eights, patterns Villoso proceeded to then stomp all over as if determined to destroy them. As he sat on the banks of the Guatiquía contemplating these critiques, he knew something needed to be done. He had to banish this protean protein that was now affecting his performance. And, slowly, a plan began to take shape. He would return to the Northern Hemisphere that November, and, citing that he wished to spend more time with Volpina over the holidays, cancel all appearances until the one scheduled in Spitz, Austria on February 14th. Then he got to work.

For what he had in mind, he knew he would need all his wits and whiskers about him. He set about growing the latter in earnest. There was one final shave to provide material for the specially designed costume he commissioned. Unwilling to forego the V's altogether, using the classic logo he had his own hair stitched front and back into a thermal wetsuit, of a length from neck to ankles and radiantly golden. Looking in the mirror, he likened himself to the Sun, a celestial body beaming his initials out for the whole universe to absorb. Things were looking up, to him at least. It was true that he and Volpina had an extended New Year's getaway booked in Vienna, but he had to be careful. Ever since the advent of the Egg Man, their relationship had been on the rocks, with her beginning to suspect there was someone else. And while the majestic Austrian capital would offer enough romance to hopefully quell her doubts, the fact that Villoso had chosen the location due to its proximity to his February plans was not quite above board. His frequent trips down the river did little to set her soul at ease. But even though he couldn't tell her why, Villoso assured his love that there was no other woman for him and that all his preoccupations would be gone come February 15th. Of this he was supremely confident.

There was a tremendous air of secrecy surrounding the Spitz exhibition. The entire world press received a summons, as well as a surprising number of chefs, chicken farmers, and descendants of the Fabergé family. None were given further information beyond a simple location, date, and time. All were intrigued. Though on the day itself Mother Nature provided an appropriate temperature to freeze the intended segment of the Danube, since the beginning of the year Villoso had Tesla-trained weather scientists on call throughout eastern Europe in case any meteorological manipulation might be required, as well as dishing out large sums of money to local officials for the necessary permits to perform his spectacular feat. On this particularly long stretch of river, a good 75 meters were sectioned off for the skating, plus an additional 50 extending on from this, within which two perfectly round circles, five feet in diameter, were cut into the ice at each end, looking like the type one would use for fishing. Villoso arrived in silence. Even if he had planned any sort of speech, he presently found himself at a loss for words, spying amidst all the eager and perplexed onlookers a human-sized egg wearing a tangerine bowler hat, its shell almost completely obscured by the newspaper it kept peering over as it leant against a dumptruck whose doors read 'HUMPHRIES CONSTRUCTION'. Despite feeling trepidation at its presence, Villoso also sensed he had this phantom on the ropes. Tracing the V sign over the one on his torso, he skated to the center of the river to begin.

With a swoop now perfected, he raised his hands out high in the air, a magnificent V that was doubled in his moustache, having gone from down to up in the midst of this gesture. Maintaining a laser sharp focus, he headed to the perimeter and began to slowly ascribe a ring around the area within which he would be performing. His blades dug deep, one after the other, to make sure the circle would be etched unbroken into the ice. As he did so, though there was initial confusion amidst the crowd, they were soon drawn in, mesmerized by his slow, steady pace, full of intent. Barely audible, he was intoning a protective incantation, a series of the word 'na', that he had recently received from a holy man in Vietnam. For prior to the holidays, he had spent his time roaming the planet, studying under occult masters in Vagharshapat, Varanasi, and various realms beyond to prepare himself for the ritual in which he was about to engage. One that would rid him of the egg entity forever. With the safety of the sacred circle now in place, the banishing began.

Back again were those same ovaled eights from the Villavicencio show, but here they served a greater purpose, Villoso shooting them daggered glances even as he traced their outlines. Once complete, he thrust himself across their interiors, arms folded in front of his chest, kicking up his legs and coming down hard on alternate ankles, X'ing out the eggs in a whirling dervish of a Russian dance. Spectators looked on in awe, clutching each other in the fear that the ice might crack as he stomped over it in every direction. Coming out of this blur of activity, Villoso launched himself into a triple axel to enormous applause as all assumed it was the finale. But no, the spotlights then swept onto the holes cut further down the waterway, Villoso already racing towards them at speed. The congregation heaved a collective gasp as that famous chest then launched into a swan dive, the type with which he was known for propelling himself across the ice. Except this time he was plummeting down past its surface. As his skates disappeared into the Danube, all held their breath, eyes soon widening at the other mouth 50 meters downriver. Exasperated fans rushed out in panic, which didn't help any as cracks proliferated under their weight. Villoso had anticipated this, though the extra security he had hired still struggled to hold back the maddened crowd.

After what seemed an eternity, two black points poked themselves up from the far hole, hairiscopes finding their bearings. All stood stunned as a bristly black V emerged in stage-managed slow motion, pulling the shimmering golden body of Villoso out of the Danube and onto the ice in triumph. The audience were unsure how to react, puzzled as to what they were actually witnessing and why. Villoso cast his gaze about before he would declare himself victorious. He had noticed, underwater, the ice begin to break above him. Swimming for his life, he steadied the rising fear, remembering what the mystics had taught him. This was a sure sign that the entity itself was cracking. At last, Villoso beamed a huge smile, for there was no sign of the Egg Man anywhere. Nor would there be from now on.

Unburdened and lighter of soul, Villoso whisked Volpina off to their hotel room and proved to her once and for all that she was the only one for him. He never bothered to explain what the whole business had been about, despite myriad attempts from journalists and fans alike to get him to clarify the proceedings. The general consensus had come to be one of pure befuddlement, with overtones of the usual anger and relief that accompanies a fellow human being safely completing a completely unnecessary stunt. True, it had been a strange and unique display, but everyone wanted to know why they had travelled so far to see it. Left to field such questions, the strain was too great for Vidal, who left Villoso's employ after being hounded for weeks to tell what he knew. This was a stroke of luck as it happened, as the stylist was quickly hired by a much wealthier and less needy client, allowing him to achieve his dream of opening a philanthropic organization supporting bassoonists in need.

The following month Villoso and Volpina flew first class to Las Vegas and were married. Catching Elvis Presley's act on their second night in town gave Villoso an idea. Waiting long enough to call it a comeback, and for all the pesky inquiries about the Spitz incident to have fizzled out, the following year Villoso had a special stage suit tailor-made for him in the style of The King, leaving of course a double-sided V open from collar to crotch and crack. The Great Villoso Revival would kick off with his very own Vegas show. But the famous skater underestimated just how cheated his fans felt over what had happened in Austria. 'Villoso in Vegas' closed after just one night, incensed attendees pelting him with rotten eggs for the entirety of his performance.

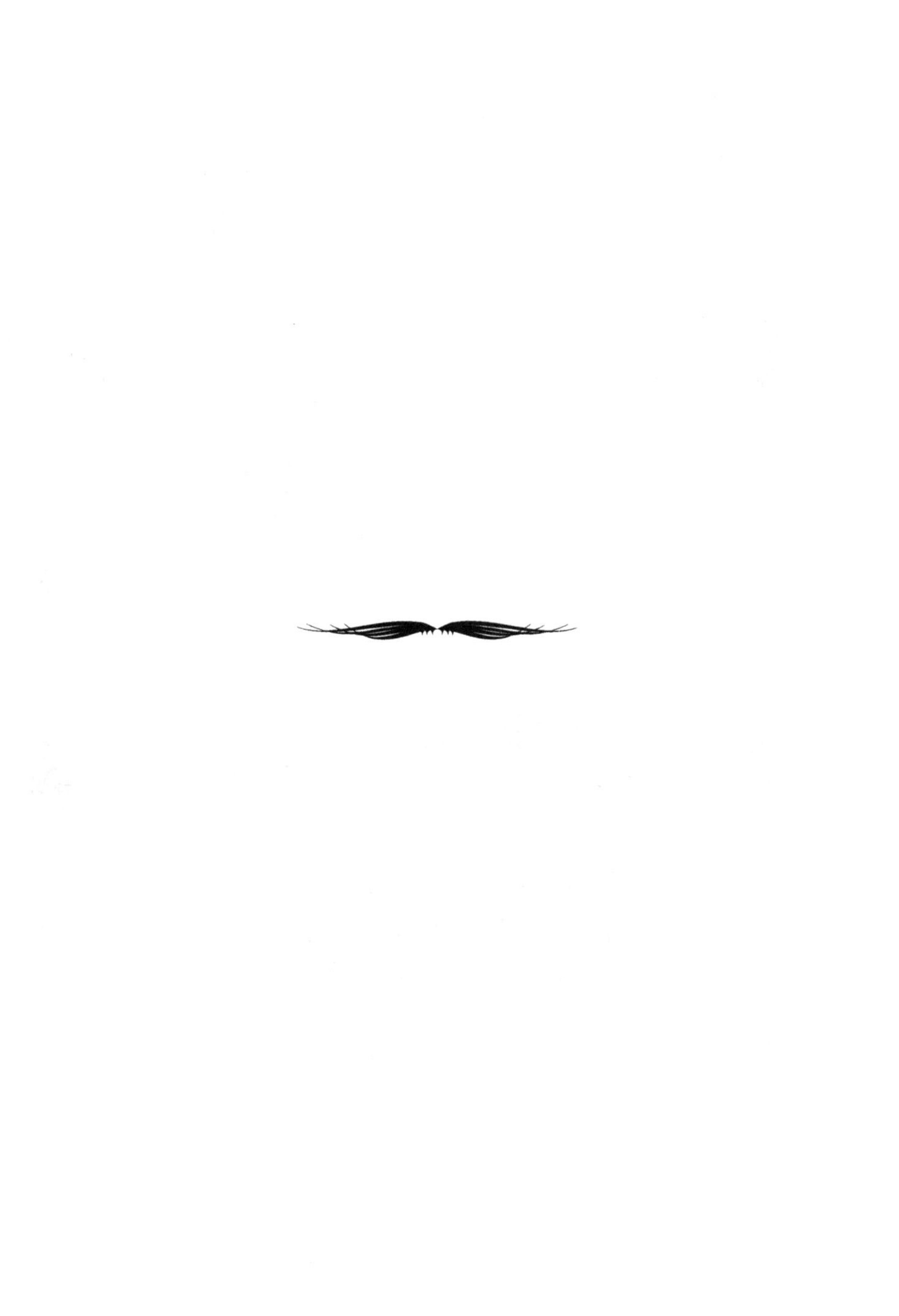

Pigheaded

No one knew where he came from, how he had learned such exquisite control, or if Hans Freeman was indeed his real name, but ever since that late July evening in 1984, he had been a force to be reckoned with. Hans simply appeared out of nowhere that day, standing by the Wolfeboro Rec air hockey table, his 6' 4" 250 pound frame glued to a spot one step back from its right hand side, extending a challenge to any and all passersby using only his eyes and a slight turn of the head. Those at the video games covertly kept tabs on the proceedings and when second string quarterback Jack Melon, eager to impress Diane Campbell who had finally agreed to go out with him, accepted Freeman's offer, a sizeable crowd closed in, emanating a collective gasp when Hans wordlessly began wrapping his lengthy goatee around the red paddle. They continued to watch in amazement as Hans then hunched over the console, eyes completely focused on the puck, head at the ready, body firmly planted in place.

It was over before anyone knew it. Hans' face lunging with his striker in one long even flow, deking and twisting to fire shot after shot, slipping in his seven in less than a minute.

Jack kicked the machine and, muttering something about 'this freak', stormed off sulkily, attempting to drag the reluctant Miss Campbell with him. Instead she stood her ground, slipped a quarter into the jukebox, and as ZZ Top's 'Legs' began to blare out of the speakers, joined the group gathering around this newcomer to congratulate him.

Hans—secretive, but not as quiet a gentlemen as his intense pre-game concentration would imply—was soon on the receiving end of many a back slap and soda pop from the wowed denizens of Wolfeboro, New Hampshire. Introductions were made, snacks were purchased, future plans discussed. Hans' play was so impressive most did not connect his name to the prowess they'd just witnessed until long after the rec center closed that night. And it wasn't until months after he started becoming famous on the competitive scene that the first disparaging comments were heard, pointing out that he actually did grip the sides of the table with his fingertips during play.

What Hans did reveal about himself that evening as the jukebox cranked out Van Halen, Duran Duran, Michael Jackson, and other much-loved hits of the day, eventually moving out to the parking lot with a cooler, boombox, and tape of Black Sabbath's *Paranoid*, was that he had just come from Climax, Georgia, having had enough of the heat and deciding to leave before it drove him crazy. Itinerant by nature, he said he'd stick around these parts for a while until the great hand of Fate moved him on. For from that he could never be free. Kicking off a tradition that would carry on through the ensuing months of his stay, as the party broke up, all raised a beverage container to toast '*cin cin*' with a smiling nod in the direction of Hans' goatee.

Every night for some weeks he would arrive at the rec center at dusk and proceed to entertain his new friends at the air hockey table. At one point or another all the locals had a go against him but it was more to see Hans in action than harboring any hopes of actually winning themselves. Occasionally they would move on to foosball, 'foozy' as it was known, where Hans would proceed to wrap his goatee around the center bar, controlling the goalie and other two attacking lines with his hands, dominating here too, and when the game was quickly won, unfurling his hair from the handle with the most elegant flick of his head, dazzling all as it careened through the air to once again hang below his chin. So captivating was Hans to be around, that if they were playing doubles—Hans obviously on the forward rods—his teammate, upon their inevitable win, would often whip off his shirt, spinning it in the air as he ran about the Rec as if it were a real soccer pitch.

Rather than having peaked down in Georgia as the name of Climax might imply, the world was only just now getting wind of Hans Freeman. The underground newspaper coverage of oddities and outliers such as himself was starting to seep into the mainstream press, audiences eager for more extreme varieties of sport. The mysterious aura surrounding Hans, with his seeming to have emerged from Climax the previous year as if out of thin air, made him a favorite for reporters and gossip columnists to alike conjecture upon. Articles appeared, helping to pack houses for competitions in locations as diverse as a farm in Brooklin, Maine, a high school gym in Angel Beach, Florida, at a Parisian fashion mag extravaganza, and on the grounds of a well-beloved castle in rural England, lines forming hours ahead of time to see this facial force. This was also the beginning of Hans' severe spinal problems. 'Never let them see you sweat', they say. Well, Hans Freeman was of the adage 'never let them see your cervical vertebrae injuries manifested in an outward neck brace.' And in the eternal clash between doctors' orders and outward appearances, Hans compromised by wearing one whenever he was alone, hidden behind closed doors with the shades securely drawn. As word of his abilities grew and he began traveling the world regularly for exhibition tournaments, Hans had a chiropractor in every port. Despite his love of Iron Maiden, Judas Priest, and an up-and-coming band called Metallica, he had to remain hyperaware and not let himself give in to the temptation to headbang along with their tunes. He unwittingly came across as 'too uptight' at concerts, though a few strokes of his goatee could usually be counted upon to change this perception to one of 'a deeply contemplative individual absorbed in the intellectual qualities of the music'.

As 1985 rolled through and the world attempted to come to grips with David Lee Roth having left Van Halen, Wolfeboro was a long ways back in Hans' rearview mirror. Heeding the frontman's message and prefiguring Gretzky's arrival in Los Angeles by three years, Hans Freeman rolled up to the oceanside air hockey tables of Santa Monica and Venice Beach's pool halls and arcades, soon finding he preferred the machines just sitting on the sand. He attributed his sanity to the dryness of the heat, though he sometimes struggled to keep a level head with all the attention his growing fame was bringing him. Hans liked the area enough to make it his home, even if tournaments kept him on the road most months of the year. Long hours in the car didn't help his neck any. By the time he next returned to LA, he could turn neither left nor right, let alone deftly maneuver an air hockey puck by the hairs of his chinny chin chin.

As luck would have it, one afternoon in a Hollywood coffeehouse as Hans was grimacing through raising a cup of joe, Doctor Wilbur Slothrop recognized him from the papers and offered a consultation free of charge. When X-rays confirmed just how severe the damage was, Hans decided to fight the pain no longer, and listened attentively as Dr. Slothrop told him about an experimental surgery in which a portion of pig spine would swap out his defective upper vertebrae.

The operation was a success and Hans recovered in time to begin training for his next big event—Newark, New Jersey's International Open. Warming up for The Brick City, he took first place in The Bluegrass State Invitational held in Straw, Kentucky, and then again at Baton Rouge's inaugural Red Striker Sudden Death Saturday. Competitive air hockey is no world to keep secrets in however, and before he even left California the press were running wild with 'Swine Spine' and 'Piggy Back' headlines, detractors everywhere now referring to Hans as 'Hooves' Freeman.

Hans, as he still called himself, rolled into Newark on the eve of a Full Moon, the International Open due to start at 5 p.m. the following day. He awoke in his hotel room and after performing his usual stretches, decided to spend the afternoon relaxing with a six pack of Coors. A mass of dark clouds were descending on the city compelling Hans to make his way over to the arena well ahead of time, picking up another sixer along the way. As the first pucks were placed, a gargantuan storm broke out over the Tri-State area, colossal thunderclaps drowning out the incessant clicking of the tables. Over the course of a few stormy hours, Hans soared through to the final round with his usual aplomb.

Walking to the console reserved for the championship match with his as-yet-unopened last beer clenched in his fist, Hans waited patiently for his opponent to arrive. And when they did, it was sensational. Blazing around the windows of the hall in a fantastic 360 degree display, lightning flared as if on a loop, crackling and zigzagging repeatedly over the entire expanse of sky. And when it was over, Hans was staring a familiar figure dead in the eyes. Now enveloped in a head of hair far more voluminous than Hans' own, with a full brown beard down past his chest, Jack Melon looked like something out of *Teen Wolf*. Smarting from his defeat three years previous in front of the lovely Diane Campbell, who never spoke to him again, Jack had left New Hampshire and honed his chops, first on the Ohio circuit, rapidly becoming a star player in Columbus and Cleveland whilst simultaneously studying economics and playing in a covers band. When he eventually caught wind that his nemesis was out in California, Jack hightailed it to Hill Valley, all the while grooming his beard longer and longer. By the time Jack tracked his foe down and settled himself in Hollywood, Hans was laying low, recovering from his spine transplant, thus necessitating a trip back east for his shot at revenge when he saw Hans' name on the Brick City roster.

Hans plucked the tab on his last can of Coors and took a long pull before beginning the ritual of wrapping his goatee around the striker. When it was tight and secure, he finished the beverage in one almighty chug, crumpled the can in his fist, and fired it into the trash receptacle directly to Jack's right. Melon flinched as it sailed past but quickly regained his composure. The two settled in and the ref moved the puck into the center. The secret of Jack's success soon became apparent. Although he could have easily tied his own hair to the mallet in an imitation of Hans, and with much to spare, Jack opted instead to hunch over the machine, letting his abundant beard hover as cover. His opponent's sightline on the disc so obscured, Jack's shoulders and eyes would initiate a series of fiery feints, diversionary jiggles, and blustering psych-outs, wearing his foe down with blinded bewilderment, until at the last second lifting his chin slightly to snipe off his shot.

Possession fell to Hans first, prompting Jack to taunt, "Go on, boy, peck like a chicken." He'd obviously not understood what Hans had been through. Nor seen *Deliverance.* Fans gathered closer, it being difficult to spot the black puck amidst all the hair. With the lightning continuing to rage outside, many swore they saw sparks flying off the paddles, and it was obvious by the postures of the players that the surface friction was something other than regulation. Neither complained, however. They were already engaged in battle. Short of a power failure—a very real possibility no one in attendance was willing to acknowledge—nothing could stop them now.

Although both men were known for annihilating their adversaries within seconds, this match lasted much longer than usual, such were the levels of skill and concentration involved. One had to hand it to Jack, he certainly played well, maneuvering his mane deftly, as according to the rulebook any contact between this and the disc would be ruled a foul. The referee was having quite a time of it, keeping tabs on hair-to-puck contact, his face held close to a table abuzz with atmospheric anomalies. To anyone else, Jack's unique style was overwhelming, but Hans showed true backbone, even if it was part porcine. The biscuit clicked and clacked to and fro, side to side, slipping under and out from Jack's beard, all the while Hans remaining focused, the crowd rapt. At 6-6, it seemed they were all levitating. Hans and Jack locked eyes, pupils burning with venom and determination. Returning Hans' gaze was Jack's mistake. Having looked away from the puck for even that split second, Jack fell for Hans' fake to the right as he banked it off the left hand wall just past the center line, completely clearing the hanging hair into Jack's goal. At just that moment, lightning flashed once more, the memory of losing in front of Diane Campbell rushed back to rumba with the despair of his current defeat, and all who caught the look on Jack's face illuminated by the electrical storm later described the curious impression of being in the presence of a lupine scarecrow. The lights in the building dimmed for a second. When they returned, Jack was gone.

Some say he decamped to the Cleveland bar band scene, others that he married his long-time therapist who he'd been seeing to deal with his rage towards Hans. There is also some evidence that Jack lingered in the area for a while and planned to run for mayor. Another popular rumor is that he commenced working on hoverboard technology with the goal of pioneering games where both player and puck stay afloat. When Jack was finally tracked down in the mid 90's, he was running a rec center aboard an old-fashioned, fully functional steam locomotive in Northern California.

What is interesting is that after the Brick City match, both Hans Freeman and Jack Melon would pursue careers that took air hockey on the move. Independently, each sought to combine the sport they loved with the long hours on the road they were putting in to play it, and thus began to believe this would be the ultimate way of competing, plus a great boon for your average traveller. Fuelled rather by expansion than negativity, Hans sought to do one better than Jack and take the enterprise to the skies. After a few more undefeated years as world champion, at a regular check-up with Dr. Slothrop, the surgeon warned that if this lifestyle continued, he would require another replacement within a few years. "Not a problem, and happy to do it," the doctor intoned. But Hans had grown used to this particular spinal companion—you never forget your first porcine transplant—and knew it was time to retire. He had other dreams, trusting that anything was possible. As he once proved to the naysayers that one could in fact play air hockey with one's face, he now set out to get his pilot's license, soon opening a premiere airline service complete with gaming tables, and proving that, indeed, pigs can fly.

The King Of Clubs

Brian Lowe-Parker cupped cold water from the faucet onto his fresh face and stared hard at the mirror, drops dripping from his nose and sliding off his chin. His eyes contained a curious mixture of despair, resilience, and general put-upon-ness. B-Low, as he was known, usually to his chagrin, had had a rough night, following an even rougher day, the latest in the ever-progressing chain of rough weekends that featured playing thirty-six holes with his boss, Augustus Masterson. Masterson never tired of the predictable 'below par' jokes whenever Brian failed to achieve this, which was usually eighteen out of eighteen times. And Brian never forgot the look of complete incomprehension on the one occasion he had attempted to explain to Masterson the origins of his family name. That his grandfather Bogdan Păr had come to America from Romania in 1897 with nothing but the hair on his head. Arriving in New York City, Bogdan soon fell in love with the spitfire Belle Lowe, and albeit starting penniless, with Belle's personality and Bogdan's patience, the two built up one of the best car services going on the Lower East Side. In an effort to ingratiate himself to his newfound countrymen, Păr dropped the accent breve and added a 'ker', the whole thing sounding both American and automotive. He also began going by 'Dan', though legally and spiritually he never dropped the 'Bog', meaning as it does 'God'. When the couple finally married, since they were such an excellent team already, it was only natural to combine their surnames as well. When Brian finished this story, Masterson silently teed up and let fly a hole in one. Rather than considering the tale to be a good luck charm, Masterson shot Brian a look of such frigid intensity that the latter never brought it up again.

Despite his grandparents' successful business, still going strong 50 years later after being passed down to his father's eldest brother Alexander, Brian found himself living upstate, working a separate job he didn't mind yet felt no real passion for either. As a mid-level executive for Calibur Advertising, he was one of those 'putting the 'U' in Caliber'. He secretly dreamt of writing novels, forging a genre that deftly combined detective fiction with gardening how-to manuals. If only he could get better at golf. It would not do to beat the boss, but oh how exhilarating it would be to give him a run for his money. It seemed, however, that Masterson had rigged the system so there was no way for Brian to even practice his swing, let alone find the time to write. Weekends were spent on the links together, where Masterson derailed all conversation even approaching technique or theory, often striking Brian in the back of the knee with a five iron if Lowe-Parker was seen working on his stance. And whatever other extra hours Brian had, Masterson filled up with further assignments.

It was on just one of these, three days later, that Brian found himself back in the domain of his ancestors, worming his way around The Big Apple. He had spent the train journey once again writing extraneous reports to the exclusion of taking in any scenery. Though having clinched the deal with his client in record time, and a return ticket for much later that evening, a free afternoon now stretched out ahead of him. And so he wandered through the streets of Greenwich Village, somewhat lost but hoping to stumble across a used book shop containing volumes of obscure horticultural expertise. Soon, although there were no such tomes in the window, a sign caught his eye—ARTHUR'S PRESERVATION AFFILIATES—and Brian felt drawn inside.

The large wooden door opened with a creak and he stepped into a lost world of antique tables, china cups, jam jars full of coin and curios—military medals mostly—a scattering of regal-looking hats sitting atop broken billiard cues, and with a plethora of long-past-relevant advertisements for new homes, pie stands, and forgotten vaudeville acts hanging on the walls and larger pieces of furniture. A cough emanated from behind the counter followed by a voice and then a figure. "Alright, mate, what brings you in today? Name is Arthur Lomax. Let me know if you see anything that tickles your fancy. I'm sure we can agree on a price. Everything's on sale, it's all gotta go. The wife just moved to Australia with our two boys, Ray and Dave, and I'm joining them next month."

Brian nodded. He had spotted two overflowing book shelves at the far end of the room and started to make his way towards them. Arthur Lomax coughed again in what he intended as a reassuring 'take your time' timbre, at which Brian's attention was diverted to his right, looking now past the proprietor and up over the counter. "Beer?" Arthur asked, noncommittally.

"Um, sure," Brian replied, his gaze remaining on what hung on the eastern wall. Arthur Lomax, polishing two pint glasses, followed Brian's sightline before he began filling these from a keg barely visible beneath the cash register. Glass full, Brian accepted it without taking his eyes off the paintings. He stood awestruck before them, repeatedly running his open palm over his clean-shaven face. In the frame on the left a dapper gentleman with a magnificent moustache was crouched over a ball amidst a copse of beech trees, one eye closed as he peered down the length of what looked like a golf club across to the far side of a frozen lake where a group of other similarly-dressed men huddled around a stake in the ground. The portrait on the right showcased this same man hovering over a small boy, letting his moustache droop down on to the stick he's teaching the child to hold.

Lomax, stroking his own extended moustache, interjected into Brian's reverie. "You're familiar with the game of kolf? Old Dutch tradition, and, as you are no doubt aware, they settled this city. New Amsterdam and all that. Though I can't imagine playing it on these streets nowadays. Someone'll steal your balls before you even get to the first hole. Funny old chap who brought that one on the right in, seemed to be in need of getting rid of it quickly, some convoluted story involving the Royal Canadian Police and an unusually large snake. I stopped him halfway through—'the less I know the better, son'. None of this kept him from jabbering though, a mile a minute, that one. For a fella with the law on his tail, he sure had time to talk. I eventually told him 'a picture is worth a thousand words, and I ain't payin' you for both'." Lomax indicated the painting on the right, "An original Raymond Kolk, though, to add to my other beauty." He motioned to the scene on the left, spilling some of his beer in the process. "Been in the family for years, centuries even. 'Joost de Heer The Elder Birdies Against An Icy Sky'. My great-grandfather brought it over from the old country, after *his* great-grandfather had brought it to England from *his* old country. Raymond Kolk's always been a huge figure in my life, named my eldest after him, and styled my tasche after Joost de Heer's." His twirled this, consideringly. "Wanted to be a painter myself until other things . . ." he swept his arm in an arc about the store, spilling even more of his beverage, ". . . got in the way."

"That portrait on the right," Lomax continued, " 'Joost de Heer The Third Takes His First Swing' reminds me of teaching young Ray the game. Say, you don't golf, do you? I've been itching to get out on the links. See, the bloke who brought in the painting also sold me this." Lomax hoisted up a sort of stick, whose dark rich texture seemed to draw in all the surrounding light in the shop, spinning this around and around, sliding it up and down in his hand as he carried on with his story.

"Now, I'd always heard rumors of the legendary Cavern Club, pulled from the rock in the cave outside St. Andrews. Ah, I can tell by the look on your face you are unfamiliar. You must not care enough for the game then, son. Allow me to set the scene. Early 15th Century, Robert The Hopeful and his trusty knight, Ted of Comfort, are out traversing the Scottish countryside. Who knows what historical significance the two of them had originally set out for, but the story goes that after making camp in a particularly damp section of woods their first night, they were each visited by visions of a cosmic cow instructing them to make haste towards a precise location. Both being sensible men, they naturally ignored the advice of any intergalactic bovine emanating from their cattle-addled unconscious and yet the following morning they ended up at the very site the creature spoke of anyway. Without much time to be flummoxed either as, peering through the trees, they saw a giant tiger prowling the perimeter of the cave's entrance. Neither could recall what the cow had said would be awaiting them inside, in fact each considered the animal's monologue to be a bit wordy, dozing off again within their own dreams, but now that they were here—"

"Wait a minute," Brian interrupted. "What was a tiger doing in Scotland?"

Lomax wrinkled his nose at the absurd query. "Guarding this cave, obviously. Now—"

"But how did it get there?"

"What a ridiculous question. I mean, at this momentous occasion they had more important matters to deal with . . . even if the tiger could tell them!"

Arthur Lomax stared his impertinent customer into submission. When he was satisfied Brian wouldn't waste any more of his time, he resumed his tale.

"Now how were they going to get past this jungle cat and into the cave is a much more reasonable puzzle to be occupying your mind. And believe me, it did theirs." Arthur spoke as if he had observed the proceedings himself rather than having heard an nth generation version of them from a dope-crazed thief. "Finally, true to his name, Ted of Comfort remembered a quantity of opium he had in his rucksack—"

"How did he get opium in Scotland in the 15th century?"

"From a Portuguese sailor." Arthur dismissed out of hand any possible retort to this, ploughing straight on, "The two soon hatched upon an idea. First, they would smoke the stash to give them a vision of what to do. Unfortunately, the vision turned out to be 'drug the tiger with the very opium they had just finished', but they did see that this plan would've worked magnificently. It would have too. And so, as they awaited the return of sobriety, the two sat down to ponder the eternal question of 'how do you trap a tiger in the woods?' Eventually, Robert The Hopeful, true to *his* name, snapped his fingers. 'I've got it! What we need is another tiger, of the opposite sex, to create a distraction.' But where would they find that in Scotland? As you so rightly pointed out a minute ago."

Brian noted Arthur's menacing tone and offered, "Maybe from another Portuguese sailor?"

"Or the same seafaring lad," Arthur shot back. "Anyways, during the course of his ruminations upon the problem, Robert recalled a foggy glimpse of a tiger hide he had once spotted for sale at a market stall in Edinburgh and in his excitement that their plans lay within reach, he became convinced that the vendor actually owned a whole shop, its multiple rooms overflowing, dedicated solely to the selling of tiger skins."

Arthur broke off to allow Brian to raise an eyebrow.

"Robert set foot apace in the direction of the great city with Ted in his wake, attempting both to keep up and to understand. When they stopped to sup from a stream, Ted was finally able to give voice to his confusion. Robert put a reassuring hand on his compatriot's shoulder. 'It's simple,' he said. 'When you don the fur, the tiger will begin to chase after you and I will rush into the cave and remove its treasure.' Ted's eyes betrayed fear and disbelief that his friend saw nothing wrong with this plan. As Robert moved to press on, Ted called out, 'But how do I escape the great beast?' Robert paused to consider this for the first time. 'If you simply toss off the pelt, the creature will go after that.'

'But what if, when it realizes the skin is just that,' Ted gulped, desperate to convey the dangers of the proposed field operation to his companion, 'it returns to its guard position and mauls your good self?'

Robert paused again. He had not thought of this either. His grand plan did not extend past the bounteous reward he would find within the walls of the cave. A treasure so vast he could open his own tiger skin shop if he so desired.

The two carried on, Ted growing ever more fretful. Until he noticed a mound of clay near the next stream they came across, its color a curious orange. They had just passed a field of cows, terrestrial this time, and a scheme of his own began to take shape in his panicking mind.

It took some convincing, plus sulking on Robert's part about the nixed trip to the city, but the two were soon leading a mud-caked cow back in the direction from whence they had come. They had spent a good hour sculpting orange stripes over the animal's brown hide, and if that other cow's monologue had rubbed them the wrong way, this animal certainly appreciated the more literal hands-on massaging. Their unpreparedness of what to do with the milk-bearer once they arrived at the awaiting mouths of both cave and tiger didn't enter the equation as once the destination was in site, the tiger was already pouncing on the unsuspecting bovine. Ted ran up a tree while Robert, almost accidentally, ended up in the cave. Crouching behind a boulder, it being too dark to see anything, he kept this position until morning. When the Sun finally shone in, Robert was baffled. Spying not treasure chest nor sacks of loot, devoid of any magical swords or sleeping maidens, what greeted his irritated gaze was this."

With great pride, Arthur twirled the baton in front of Brian's face. He waited a good ten seconds for any look of awe to materialize there. With none forthcoming, he continued. "This. What I now hold in my hands, before your very eyes. What became known as The Cavern Club, its true name lost to the sand traps of time. But believe you me, whomever wields such a stick is given innumerable powers over that little white ball we all seek to sink."

Despite himself, Brian felt drawn to the artcfact, given to visions of how these properties might alter his life for the better. He reached out to stroke it. Arthur indulged him.

"Feel how smooooth that is. Obviously forged from different strains of bestial hair, probably what gives it such adaptability on the course. The head and most of the staff appears to be a mix of otter fur and sea lion whiskers. Which stands to reason, they are the longest in the animal kingdom. But see this white line running through, circling up and around? Seems purely decorative, though you never know. I'd bet money that's artic fox hair. And the handle is—" Arthur held the rod arms' length away from his face, squinting like a jeweler examining a diamond "- Iberian, maybe Eurasian, lynx. Chap who brought it in says he never lost a game with it in his hands. I've been meaning to—"

"What happened next?"

"What do you mean?"

"When this Robert found himself in a cave with this strange object and a tiger waiting outside?"

"Oh. That." Arthur let out a deep breath. "Right . . . Well, this," tapping the head of the club into his palm, "was stuck in a stone, you see. And Robert couldn't tell if the true treasure was on the end of it, lodged into that rock. So he put one foot on the boulder for extra purchase, and pulled with everything he had. It came out remarkably easily, as if it had been reunited with its true owner. This line of thinking was confirmed when he walked outside brandishing his new find and the tiger knelt down before him."

"Knelt down? A tiger?"

"More of a bow, really. But yes. And then disappeared, its duty done."

"Aha. And this Ted of Comfort?"

"Came down from the tree and was obviously overjoyed about the tiger being gone. And the discovery of the club, of course."

"Of course. And what did they do next?"

"Made their way to St. Andrews. And on into the great golf lore of history. But look, let's not waste any more time. If we leave now, we can still make nine holes over at Forest Park, try this baby out."

"You haven't tried it out yet?

"Course I have. Improved my game in ways I wouldn't have thought possible. I meant for you."

"Oh." Brian decided not to question Arthur any further. No matter how far-fetched this story seemed and how unlikely such a relic would end up here in 1950s New York, if it could shave down his golf score and set him free from the tyranny of Augustus Masterson then he was willing to give it a whirl.

The two strolled outside and hailed what turned out to be a Lowe-Parker taxi, Brian's fortunes already changing. The driver also happened to be a distant cousin and refused any fare for the ride. A lucky break, as Arthur's air made it apparent that Brian would be picking up the tab for everything. They pulled up to the pro shop just in time and alternated holes with the club. In fact, it was the only one they used when it was their turn. Brian marveled at its versatility, and how much better he was playing. Along the way Arthur gave him pointers about grip, stance, and swing, which Brian was able to incorporate almost immediately. How freeing it was to be allowed a moment to do so. With the score tied and both well under par after the eighth hole, Arthur leaned in on his pitch. He had let Brian tee off first which meant that the stick would return to Brian for this last hole. "So what do you think of her?"

Brian was unable to conceal his admiration. "She's a beauty."

Arthur nodded in agreement. "She sure is. It saddens me to have to part with her but, like I said, I'm leaving for Australia in a month and who knows if customs will even allow such a piece in the country, exotic wildlife and all that. I've been hoping to find a good home for her and I could tell by the way that you were admiring my Raymond Kolks that you are a man with a wealth of taste. If you're interested . . ." He let it dangle.

"Yes?"

"I could let you have her for, say . . . $8,000."

Brian gasped.

"Okay, okay, seven. But only if you promise to take care of her."

Brian had not expected any of this. The offer or the exorbitant price. Yet he could see that it was worth it, that with such magic in his hands he would be well on his way to the life of his dreams. The deal was concluded as soon as Brian won the 9th hole, and game, by one point. Each considering it a stroke of luck. The two proceeded to a celebratory dinner, on Brian of course, before they were to part ways. Wishing Lomax all the best Down Under, Lowe-Parker decided to walk back to the station, making his way through streets covered in Men At Work, High Voltage, and church signs. The late evening train was none too crowded and once his ticket had been inspected, Brian opted not to sit down. Instead, standing tall in the aisle, he hovered over his newly acquired talisman, practicing all Arthur had taught him about technique.

Come the following Saturday, it was time to put things to the test. How would Brian fare against his boss? During the course of the week his grip rarely left the club—fondling it with his free hand over dinner, sleeping with it next to him in bed, its head perched upon the specially fluffed pillow, even having to stop himself from bringing it in the shower with him. Smuggled into work in a poster tube, he hid the container below his desk whenever anyone walked by. Throughout all this, Brian could sense his feelings changing. He expanded his ambitions from simply wishing to put an end to Masterson's 'below par' jokes to no longer caring if beating his boss on the golf course would mean the end of his job. He wanted, *craved*, the authority winning would give him. So much so, that on occasion he felt himself merging with the Cavern Club, stepping into the power it radiated. He hadn't noticed that he'd gone all week without shaving until Masterson scolded him as they were leaving work on Friday. "You better buy yourself a new razor before tee time tomorrow, boy." Brian complied, but instead of revisiting the fresh cheeks and smooth upper lip he had exhibited his entire adult life, that morning in front of the mirror, his new purchase in his left hand and safety blade in his right, he opted to shape the emerging hair into sleek bars hanging down from each side of his mouth. Wiping the excess shaving cream off with the head of the club, he felt its approval.

Masterson greeted Brian in the bar with a look beyond exasperation. "Where's your bag, boy?"

Brian didn't rise to the bait. Keeping cool, he nonchalantly slid the cotton tiger print cover off the only club he was carrying. "This is all I need."

"You must be out of your fool mind."

Masterson may have thought Brian crazy, but this was qualified once they began to play. After Brian's three strokes on the recommended four of the first hole, Masterson's face turned a sickly shade of blueberry, a lump bulging in his throat as if a 'below par' joke he could not bring himself to modify had gotten stuck there.

Although his complexion soon backed off from the purple end of the spectrum, with Brian ahead by four strokes, Masterson's throat and cheeks barely contained several veins on the verge of explosion. The rage didn't help his game any. He stormed off the green after the 18th hole, returning to point a shaking forefinger in Brian's face. "Tomorrow. We rematch."

That Sunday morning Brian shaved again. His hair was coming in faster and fuller, and he wanted to highlight his nascent tasche by bringing it into relief next to bare skin. As he gazed in the mirror, running The Cavern Club over his fleshy cheeks, he felt more confident than he ever had in his life.

Following Masterson's three attempts to putt in his ball on the 9th hole, frustration further aggravating the score to Brian's now whopping nine stroke lead, Masterson grabbed the magical staff and snapped it over his knee. He then threw it on the ground to stomp with both feet repeatedly, knees up to his neck as he jumped higher and higher, shouting in irritated resentment all the while. The two did not speak as they made their way to the next tee, Brian having calmly picked up the rod and smoothed its resilient fibers back into formation.

Finally, as they were approaching the 17th green, the entire intervening time having been passed in silence, Masterson cleared his throat. "Where did you get that thing?"

Brian paused. "It was a gift." In a way, like with most things in their profession, this was true. He had bought the club believing it would enhance his game, but he had no idea the improvements would be so vast. And it was a gift from God his finding Arthur Lomax's shop in the first place.

Masterson scrunched up his face. He was afraid of this. "Can you not find out where they procured it? What is it made of anyway?"

To this Brian felt he could be truthful. "To my untrained eye, it seems like a mixture of otter fur and sea lion whiskers. And I'd bet the white is artic fox." Truthful for the most part. He had no idea why he left out the lynx hair, but he felt it vital to do so.

"You wouldn't consider selling it, would you?"

"Sir, it was a gift." And although he did not intend such a devastating punctuation to his statement, Brian then let loose a hole in one.

The following weekend, on the same hole, with Brian's tasche in full effect, Masterson repeated his offer. Brian again firing off an ace. This went on for a month, with each Sunday Masterson sweetening the pot. First offering Brian a promotion, in addition to what he'd pay for the club.

"This will come with more work?"

"Naturally, to accompany the prestige . . ." Masterson unaware that Brian could see through his scheme to keep him occupied.

Longer lunches were then thrown into the mix. Hours Brian could use to write, true, but since his encounter with Arthur Lomax he'd learned to better manage his days, finding time to stop and smell the roses, and other flora, so exactingly manicured about the course. Scents that sent him into reveries about the books he would one day write, jotting down notes on the back of blank scorecards whenever Masterson's head was turned. A company car was put on the table, an apartment in the city, a manservant, all of which Brian turned down, not wishing to sell himself into more corporate slavery.

After six weeks, Masterson shocked him while walking from the 9th to the 10th hole by demurely asking if he might be allowed to try this remarkable object. By now Brian's moustache was flowing past his chin. Stroking this, he consented. Sure enough, Masterson's game instantly improved. Simply placing his hands on the club calmed him greatly, allowing him to focus. Finishing out the 10th hole four strokes to Brian's three, Masterson flat out refused to relinquish his grip for the rest of the round. At the 15th, the two were neck and neck. Brian only leading by what he had accrued before Masterson took possession of the legendary stick. Though he still ended up losing by that amount, Masterson was so giddy at his change in fortune coming off the last hole that he nearly knocked a lady into its lake.

While with the Cavern Club in his hands, Masterson was cool and composed, without it he was like a drug fiend aching for his next fix. He showed up on Brian's front step at 11 p.m. that Wednesday night, asking to hold it for just one minute. With a heavy sigh, Brian went and got his companion out of bed, the fever fading from Masterson's eyes as soon as its hairs slid into his palm. As 5 o'clock rang that Friday, Brian was again visited by his boss, this time looking as serious as he had ever seen him.

"I have a proposition for you. Since you've been so reluctant to part with that thing, let us play tomorrow. The full eighteen. We will both use it, for every hole. If I win, the club is mine. You will surrender all claims to it. But if you win, I will give you the company. Calibur Advertising will be yours to do with as you please."

Brian sat down in shock. The club coming into his possession had bestowed a grace, previously unknown, over every aspect of his life. None more evident than in the challenges of dealing with Masterson. Could he really risk losing all that? Calibur Advertising was a very profitable enterprise, as owner he would accumulate enough money to retire early and write those long-dreamt-of books, in a big house with an English garden and all the topiarial inspiration he could desire—

tangerine trees, strawberry fields, California grass. He pondered for a moment.

"So I would be your boss?"

"Yes, I suppose you would."

At which, Brian stood up and held out his hand to accept Masterson's offer.

The two met at the top of the front nine the next morning at precisely 10 a.m. with the one club between them. Masterson insisted on teeing off first, being as he was Brian's guest, using his equipment. Each time it traded hands, Brian shivered inside, Masterson all too eager to grab, his eyes delighting at every touch. Most disconcerting was that Masterson's normal wag of the hips as he settled into his stance had now accrued into a full-on hula dance.

The two played their very hearts out, as if their lives depended on it. Both stayed well below par, mostly alternating winning holes, with scores averaging out to keep them tied. Then just as Masterson chipped the ball over the course's infamous desert on the 14th hole and was walking up to the green, it happened. A giant red buck materialized at the edge of the rough, its eyes laser-focused on what Masterson was holding. A few witnesses would later claim there was a large spotted cat perched atop its back as a sort of rider, though all Brian saw was the deer bolt across the fairway, its ferocious jaws snatching The Cavern Club out of Masterson's hands before bounding off into the afternoon Sun.

Masterson stood gobsmacked. He would later tell of the power behind the animal's bite and how he feared for his life. Brian was no less distraught. After letting a few parties play through, however, the two men decided to finish their game.

There was no longer a question of stakes but rather of honor. They hired one set of clubs to share and carried on. Brian fingering his moustache, nervous from not having touched a regular wood or iron in months. Yet on the remaining four holes, he swung admirably. As it did with the hairs on his face, The Cavern Club had brought out the best in him, qualities that would remain on the surface forever after. Fittingly, for two men who had been through such an ordeal together, the game ended in a tie.

Brian Lowe-Parker and Augustus Masterson felt a temporary bond, often par for the course with parties accosted by giant beasts, but unlike Robert The Hopeful and Ted of Comfort who worked together from the get-go, after the initial shock faded, this event only served to drive a wedge further between them. The invitations to the country club ceased. And soon Brian left Masterson's employ as he had always intended. This now ex-Calibur man got a job driving for his uncle's firm in the city, though try as he might he could never quite locate the site where ARTHUR'S PRESERVATION AFFILIATES had been. There were no records of an Arthur Lomax in any of the old phone books. Living in a cheap room in Carroll Gardens, however, Brian finally found the time to write. Blending his own experience with what he'd heard from that curious shopkeeper, he reimagined the tale of the club, changing the roles within the cast of creatures, with the deer now guardian and namesake of such a treasure. His debut novel, *Across The Universe*, the first of the Arthur Lomax series, sold millions worldwide, readers readily connecting with the adventures of this brilliant, and brilliantly moustached, art collector/kolf enthusiast/horticulturist/detective. *Across The Universe* chronicles the search for two young hopefuls, Bob and Ted, who mysteriously vanish after receiving messages from a cosmic tiger. Lomax gets a hold of these communiqués via an ex-cop on the run, deciphering them to reveal reports of a giant red deer who ceaselessly roams the Earth with a staff of power betwixt its teeth. If a fortunate soul can wrest the rod from its jaws, all their innermost desires will come true. Legend has it that the buck will remain a solitary rover until it succeeds in carrying out this task, only then will its own true doe appear, beckoning him to the blessed lands of the South. Bob and Ted were last glimpsed dressed as cattle near the Canadian border, covertly planting a long and winding labyrinth of roses and ivy in the hopes of trapping this magical beast and thus stealing the lonely Hart's Club. And they might have done so, had it not been for a phantom feline rider with mechanical limbs and an arsenal of flowers, whose own escapades make up the majority of Brian's next novel, *Robopus' Garden*.

Make Mine A Double

The Hair Of The Dog Drinking Competition requires a personal invitation from a member of Bassett, CA's Russell family. While there are plans to relax the policy on spectators attending the annual event without an embossed and signed summons, it goes without saying that participants are additionally expected to possess a moustache of a certain length. There is no set measurement in the rule book, only that the drinker be able to tie their tasche around a shot glass in order to hoist it to their own lips.

What began in the late 19th century as a way of passing the time when the extended Russell clan gathered for holidays soon gained momentum, with siblings, cousins, various 'in-laws', and several dubious connections without even a whiff of regulation facial hair, arriving eager to play on Christmas, New Year's, St. Patrick's Day, Easter, The Fourth Of July, and Thanksgiving. As the years went on, relatives welcomed the addition of Memorial and Labor Day to the calendar, any excuse for a picnic, and informal impromptu double-headers often extended New Year's Eve into the following afternoon for those who desired to stomach more, or harbored delusions that they could.

Bemoustached friends began to be invited, and John 'Jack' Russell, at whose ancestral home the event was held, soon felt that in the spirit of fairness—for now boasting such an extensive rotating cast, surely no non-blood relative would be in attendance at every familial function—the 'official' contest should be held but once per year. At first Jack considered his birthday—June 19th—but then reasoned this might give him an unfair advantage. Next he contemplated ratifying the loose proceedings that occasionally occurred on January 1st, as the numerals I I, written without any sort of extraneous punctuation between month and day, when flipped on their side look rather like a straight moustache set in determination over a firm mouth. But given that these celebrations at the Russell family seat, even well before the singing of 'Auld Lang Syne', routinely featured the wringing out of vomit-and-alcohol-soaked garments, ofttimes in the nude no less, Jack was little inclined to add to the carnage. And January 3rd, or I 3, was too close to be free from any lingering hangovers. After hours spent brooding over flip-flopped calendar pages, rolling the more ethereal qualities of each date around the inner recesses of his mind, Jack was beginning to believe all lost as he breezed past August's National Watermelon Day, Poet's Day, and the children heading back to school, on into September, the month so celebrated by Kurt Weill, with its World Coconut and National Wildlife Days, when his eyes alighted upon on the number 6. Yes, the 6th of September. For when written as 9-6, it appeared to be the head-on view of a face, not just the mouth and its accompanying locks, but a full visage with the dash delineating the axis of the tasche, the curves its flowing strands, tied around those loops which were of course the shot glasses themselves sailing through the air. How much more truthfully this depicted the fray than his own 6 I 9, which would have to be rotated 90 degrees to give the same effect, and even then appeared too restrained, 9-6 really showing the glasses and hair in action. Jack marveled at this interplay of digits and the way it mirrored the momentum. And suddenly he had an idea.

After the infamous third official contest of 1937, Russell would claim that the astonishing twist he performed simply came to him on a whim. In actuality he had been preparing the maneuver since that day in front of his desk calendar, well ahead of even the inaugural tournament. Since the game's inception, the order of play was to tie the strands of one's moustache around a shot of spirit, the brand of which was agreed upon by all contenders before the festivities began in an effort to keep blood alcohol levels uniform, and throw back one's head whilst aiming to hurl the highball to one's lips, thusly imbibing. Of course much drink was spilt, towels kept at the ready as if this were a particularly brutal boxing match, but a judge, not necessarily sober in the early days, presided over the table to rule if a significant amount of liquid had entered the contestant's mouth to be awarded a point. Results were tallied over an evening and a winner summarily announced. However, as advancements are often the product of outsider ingenuity, during the continuing unofficial holiday shenanigans, as well as by those friends of the family working on their own innovations throughout the course of the year, showmanship became so embedded into the proceedings that, by the first event proper, additional guidelines had to be established.

If, after heaving by hair the shot glass into the air, one could then, say, bounce the receptacle off one's chin for a second volley prior to its contents spilling onto an awaiting tongue, such a successful trick shot, and any like it, would be awarded 10 points. Flair was encouraged but not so much that a steady drinker could not still prove victorious over bravado repeatedly failing to connect with its intended mouth.

And so it was during a late round of The Third Annual Hair Of The Dog Drinking Competition, with scores running roughly identical, that the great patriarch Jack Russell himself shocked and amazed all in attendance by holding up his hand for silence. With the respect that was his due, a hush rapidly descended over the audience, enraptured by what they next saw taking place at the table. Russell, with measured care, knowing he was two points off the lead and that now was the perfect time to unleash his great secret weapon, reached for *two* shot glasses from the awaiting stockpile and, to audible gasps, began to tie the left flank of his bountiful brown moustache around one, then, separately, affix his right around the other. A double—whether considered too perilous, punishing, or just plain folly—had never previously been attempted. Eyes bulged out of spectators' heads as Russell threw back his, sending the brimming vessels heavenwards, arcing through a seemingly luminescent sky, to pause for a second asparkle before toppling over in unison, the amber liquid of fine 10 year old Scotch that had been specifically chosen for this round cascading down into Russell's wide-open gob. Such was the beauty of the display, that a brief moment of quietude was awarded the trick as all stood too mesmerized to yet applaud. The receptacles then descending for the by now familiar bounce off the chin, this time, post-pour, to travel further northwards landing upended over Russell's upturned eyes. The crowd could not believe their own. Wild cheers erupted in the arena and play was paused as the judge and other prominent contest figures formed a make-shift high council to discuss how to score such a feat. The 20 points of 10 per glass didn't seem to capture the sheer vitality of the move. After just a brief respite, the drinkers growing restless, it was decided to add 25 to Jack's tally, giving a bonus for boldness and style. A triumph of this kind was hardly to be topped, and no one dared mimic Jack's glory, for even in their advanced states of inebriation the players knew that to attempt a similar stunt would require powers of coordination well beyond their current means, but glasses were summarily attached to tasches and everyone began trying to rack up further rounds of 10. Much facial bruising would be seen the next day, and even though some came dangerously close to Jack's lead, those extra five for flair held out to usher him to victory. Amidst all the clamor, Russell was hoisted onto shoulders and carried outdoors, where celebrations continued long into the morning hours.

Despite being somewhat arbitrarily awarded, panache points really seem to make the game, and the revised scoring system still stands to this day. As progress often does, these maneuvers push the numbers very high. Longstanding Russell family associate Spud 'Hurricane' Peacock currently holds the record of landing four doubles in one evening, winning with an impressive 104, the closest competitor coming in at 88 after completing three deuces of his own. J.K. 'Slip' Knotts also pulled off the hat trick but was on the receiving end of a recent ruling that if you attempt a histrionic double and miss, you also lose 25 points. There are even some factions—intent on returning the sport to a more pure consumption of alcohol—that are petitioning to then render you automatically disqualified.

Innovation is a vital part of any process and although, for those who were there that night, the sheer excitement of Jack Russell's antics have yet to be matched, kudos must be given to the players who have introduced further exciting spectacles into the proceedings. After news of Queen Elizabeth II's coronation in 1953, Buzzo Diamond honored the event with 'The Crown', a move whose performance only elicited the 10 points for a single glass maneuver, but its majesty was nonetheless appreciated by all, greeted with royal looks of beneficence in inebriated eyes. And in the post-Christmas excitement of 1964's *Rudolph The Red-Nosed Reindeer* television special, during the New Year's Eve festivities, Donald Blitzer called for Campari and careened the carmine shot up to sit upon his nose, all in attendance doubling over with laughter while, keeping contents aloft, Blitzer spun 360 degrees to show the whole room before tipping it over onto a tongue stretched to slay. Frankie Hollywood's elegant 'Teardrop', whereupon he catches the shot glass square against his forehead, tips it forward, and lets the liquid slide in a stately procession from the rim of his eye down a slippery cheek, to then wince into his mouth. Funnily enough, the move was originally a double, 'Teardrops', but winning the 1985 contest with it, Hollywood realized a single stream was more aesthetically pleasing than full-on sorrow, and thus competition rank took second place to his art. And finally, just last year, Russell's twin grandsons, Conor and Conan, though—there being two of them—only acceptable in exhibition matches, after quickly learning to feed each other tasche-tied drinks across the table, succeeded in 'The Cross Eyes', expanding their grandfather's original feat into an intertwining move whose mechanics have been much discussed since the very day after Russell's wondrous display.

Allen Crawford is an illustrator, artist, designer, and writer. Allen wrote, illustrated, and designed *The Affected Provincial's Companion* (Bloomsbury 2006), which was optioned for film four times by Johnny Depp's production company, Infinitum Nihil. His second book, *Whitman Illuminated: Song of Myself* (Tin House 2014), is an illustrated edition of Walt Whitman's epic poem. The entire 256-page book was written by hand. It won numerous awards, including a Gold Medal from the Society of Illustrators, and "Best of Show" in 3x3's International Show No.12. His most recent book, *A Wild Promise* (Tin House 2023) is an illustrated celebration of the Endangered Species Act.

Aug Stone is a writer, musician, and comedian. His 2023 novel, *The Ballad Of Buttery Cake Ass*, was one of Vulture's Best Comedy Books Of The Year. Aug is also author of the memoir *Nick Cave's Bar* and the comedy novel *Off-License To Kill*, and his journalism has appeared in *The Quietus*, *The Comics Journal*, *Under The Radar*, and many more sites and magazines. Aug was a founding member of H Bird and The Soft Close-Ups, and has played in countless other bands. He performs comedy as absurdist stream-of-consciousness raconteur, Young Southpaw.

Printed in the USA
CPSIA information can be obtained
at www.ICGtesting.com
CBHW030847130324
5199CB00006B/6

9 781952 386800